Caster & Flee

THE
CASE
OF THE
MASQUERADE
MOB

PAULA HARMON
LIZ HEDGECOCK

WHITE
RHINO
BOOKS

For Gertrude Bell,
traveller, politician, writer, linguist,
mountaineer…

Chapter 1
Connie

I stifled an exclamation as a figure in the doorway threw the room into shadow. 'I thought I might find you here.' Albert smiled at me from the doorway, then came into the nursery.

I looked up, half-guiltily. 'I sent Nanny to the kitchen for a break.'

'Indeed.' Albert stooped to peep inside the crib where baby Bee slept peacefully, her tiny fists above her head and a satisfied look on her face. 'Have you been wearing the poor thing out, Connie?'

I grinned at him. 'More like the other way round. She plays until she's hungry, and feeds until she's completely knocked out.'

Albert reached down as if to stroke her cheek, but his hand stopped perhaps two inches short as if he were scared of what might happen.

'She won't bite,' I said, stroking the little pink cheek

myself. 'Though she has got two teeth.'

'Has she?' Albert looked rather horrified. 'Is that normal?'

'Apparently.' Bee wrinkled her nose, so I took my hand away. 'Nanny says that means it's time to wean her.'

'Mmm,' Albert said, his eyes on the baby. 'How old is she now?'

'Six months and a week,' I said, without thinking.

'Yes,' said Albert. 'I suppose it is about time.'

I tried not to appear too surprised at this sudden display of child-rearing expertise. 'I can still feed her, even if she is going to start eating proper food.'

A mischievous light sparkled in Albert's blue eyes. 'If she's anything like her parents, she'll be on three-course meals before she's a year old. Mrs Jones will have her work cut out.' Then the light softened. 'But it will be nice to have you — well — back.'

I glanced up at him. 'I haven't been away.'

Oh, but I had. I could barely believe I was the same person who had gone adventuring with Katherine and done all manner of strange things in the name of justice. That belonged to another life. So did the days of balls and parties. My world had narrowed to our house, the park, and a few friends' houses (provided they didn't mind babies), and was almost entirely focused on a little bundle of black hair, blue eyes and giggles. And that was the way I liked it.

***

The process had begun when I was six months pregnant, and Dr Farquhar had decreed that it was time for bed rest.

'But I'm perfectly well,' I had protested.

Dr Farquhar frowned over his pince-nez at me. 'I want you to stay that way.'

Unfortunately Dr Farquhar had also passed his prescription on to Albert, who insisted that I comply. 'You can't be too careful, Connie,' he had said, and the pain in his eyes had given me no choice but to agree.

So the next day, for the last time, Tredwell drove me to the Department. As he handed me down from the carriage (something which had become increasingly necessary as my pregnancy advanced), I looked up at the tall, impassive building which had seemed so frightening on my first day. Would I ever enter it again?

Katherine's brows knitted as she crossed the threshold and saw me already seated at my desk. 'You're . . . early?'

'I know,' I replied, hoping that I didn't look as hangdog as I felt. 'I have something to tell you.'

She grinned. 'You're not pregnant, are you?' She crossed to the filing cabinet and took out the little portable stove we used for tea.

'Oh, do be quiet. You're on the right lines, though.' I gathered up my courage into a tight ball. 'Dr Farquhar says it's time for me to leave. I'm giving you my notice. Effective today.'

Katherine took a step back, as if I had pushed her. 'Oh.' She leaned against the filing cabinet, watching me. 'Of course I knew you'd have to leave at some point. I just didn't think it would be so sudden.'

'I'm sorry.' I felt my face heating up as if Katherine had set me going instead of the stove.

Katherine delved into the cabinet for the teapot. 'Will you come back?' Her voice, from within the drawer, sounded strangely echoey, and I had a vision of Katherine all alone in the big office, waiting for me to return.

I wanted to say 'Yes, of course I shall.' That would make Katherine smile again, and we would have a nice last day together in the office.

'I don't know.'

Work at the Department had become — not exactly routine, but restricted, at least for me. Mr Maynard had come up with a new area of investigation for us, but inevitably, as I grew larger and more conspicuous, Katherine ended up doing more and more of the active work. My role was office-based; reading, researching and talking through Katherine's findings with her.

'I'll miss you, Connie,' said Katherine, then said nothing more until she brought me a cup of black tea, not too strong.

'Perhaps you could hire someone else,' I said, as brightly as I could manage.

'Perhaps,' she said, and returned to her desk.

I had, mostly, complied with doctor's orders. I had reclined on the bed or the sofa and read, and received a few visitors. Increasingly, though, my mind was occupied with the imminent event. I was not scared, despite my sister Jemima's detailed account of little Arthur's arrival. If anything, I wanted to get it over with and emerge from my little prison upstairs.

Dr Farquhar assured me afterwards that I had had an easy delivery, which made me feel intense sympathy for any mother who had had a difficult one. My nerves were not improved by the heavy tread of Albert's father, pacing in the corridor outside; but how could I ask that he cease, or go somewhere else? I had heard his voice downstairs when he arrived — 'How is Mrs Lamont? Is everything all right? Is it going as it should?' — and beneath the slightly hectoring manner was a note of blind panic. He must have set out the moment he heard the news.

Then it was all over. 'It's a girl!' proclaimed Dr Farquhar, and I was shown a scarlet-faced, screaming, white-wrapped bundle, which was quickly whisked from my presence. And while I was buzzing with excitement, and longed to see Albert and hold my baby, Dr Farquhar insisted that I sleep. How could I sleep, after *that*?

I insisted on an audience with my husband and my daughter the next morning. Mrs Kincaid, Dr Farquhar's recommendation, who had told me rather forcefully that she was always addressed as 'Nanny', had been on standby for two weeks. She seemed ferociously glad to have something to do at last — so much so that I had to ask, again rather forcefully, to be allowed to hold my own child. She was a little less red than the last time I had seen her, and now I could make out a black fuzz on her head. When her eyes opened they were slate-blue, and the same shape as Albert's. I tried to remember all the girls' names we had thought of, and scrutinised her to see which one might fit.

'Father's over the moon,' said Albert, who looked exhausted. 'He wanted to offer his congratulations in person, but Nanny thought it would be too much for you.'

I looked at Nanny with a new respect. She caught my

eye, and looked back steadily. 'I suppose you'll be wanting to try and feed her,' she said, her slight Scots burr becoming a little more pronounced.

'Yes, please.' If Nanny did roll her eyes, it was very subtle.

While my idea of how the process worked was purely theoretical, baby knew exactly what to do, and with some manoeuvring (during which Albert turned his back, and Nanny tutted audibly), soon she was feeding contentedly, her tiny fingers patting me. I was absurdly proud of myself, and I could feel my shoulders losing their tension.

'Beatrix,' I said. 'Bee for every day.'

Albert sat on the bed next to me. 'And Charlotte, for Mama.'

'Yes, of course.' I adjusted the baby's — *Beatrix's* — shawl. 'And we'll have to include Euphemia, for Mother.' I paused. 'And what about Katherine?'

'I'd like to,' said Albert. 'But it's a big name for such a mite.'

'She'll grow into it,' I said. 'What if we had all boys apart from Bee?'

Albert wrinkled his nose. 'I suppose it's possible. Go on then, stick K in there.'

'Hullo, Beatrix Charlotte Euphemia Katherine Lamont,' I said. Bee hiccupped, but apart from that seemed to take it rather well. 'I've put them in alphabetical order so that no one can argue.'

***

Back in the present, Nanny entered the nursery without knocking. 'There's a caller downstairs for you, ma'am. A

Miss Frobisher.'

I frowned. When was the last time I had seen Maisie? Not since well before Bee, when I had picked Maisie's brains about mesmerists. I considered asking Nanny to step downstairs and offer my apologies, as it wasn't my at-home afternoon, but…

'We'll both go,' said Albert. 'I haven't seen Maisie for ages.'

Nanny stood by the crib and watched us out of the nursery. 'I think Nanny is suspicious of me,' I murmured, as we walked downstairs, side by side.

Albert mused for a moment before answering. 'I think she's used to doing her job without having a mother under her feet wanting to do half of it herself.'

'She'll have to get used to it,' I said, as we reached the hall.

'Connie, is that you?' Maisie came to meet us and held her hands out to me. 'You're looking very well, considering.'

'Considering what?' I said, laughing.

'Well, you've had a child. I expected you to have your hair half down and no figure left at all.'

'Thank you so much, Maisie.' I couldn't help but smile. Maisie's sharp observations were a refreshing change from the cautions and warnings which seemed to be my lot on most days. 'To what do I owe the pleasure?'

Maisie scrutinised me, then laughed herself. 'I was given four tickets for an event, and it occurred to me that it might be your sort of thing.'

I led the way into the drawing-room and ordered tea.

'And what is my sort of thing?' I asked, once Nancy had departed.

'Not stuffy,' said Maisie, pulling two gilt-edged cards from her bag. 'Not part of the Season.'

'Oh, the Season,' I groaned. 'So it isn't that, but what is it?'

Maisie passed me the cards. '*A White Masked Ball in Aid of the All Hallows Orphanage. Costumes on the Theme Welcome. Expect the Unexpected,*' I read. 'That doesn't tell us much. Who gave you the tickets?'

'You're very suspicious, Connie,' said Maisie, looking rather offended. 'I thought you'd be thrilled to get out of the house. You're too pale.'

'I shall be just right for a white masked ball, then,' I said, giving a card to Albert.

'I got the tickets from Toby Langlands,' said Maisie. 'He's involved in some way. I think he was tired of being snubbed at dances all season.'

'We should go, then,' said Albert. 'Do you have an escort, Maisie?'

Maisie's nose elevated itself a good few inches. 'Of course,' she replied. 'I'm having a pair of costumes made specially.'

'But what about —'

'Bee will be perfectly all right,' said Albert. 'Nanny and the night nurse will be on duty.' Albert had insisted on a wet-nurse for night feeds. 'She won't even know you're not there.'

I'll know I'm not there, I thought, but kept it to myself. 'Do you want to go?' I asked.

'Yes,' said Albert. 'I want to take my wife out on the town for a change.'

I sighed. 'Very well.' I checked the date on the card. 'I'll see what Maria can do for us with three weeks' notice.'

'Excellent!' said Maisie. 'It will be fun to see you treading on each other's feet again.'

'And we can try to work out who your mystery escort is,' I replied. 'I simply can't wait.'

'It will be fun,' said Albert, once Maisie's carriage had clattered away.

'Perhaps,' I said. 'It will certainly be something different, anyway. I just hope I can fit into a formal dress.'

'You'll be fine.' Albert's arms snaked round my waist. 'Or you could always go as a white billiard ball.'

'As could you,' I said, poking the middle of Albert's waistcoat, where his stomach protruded perhaps an eighth of an inch more than it had when we first met.

'Too much comfortable living and not enough exercise, you see.' Albert smiled. 'You'll have to put me through my paces at the ball, Connie.'

'Indeed I shall,' I said, and kissed him.

CHAPTER 2
Katherine

All eyes were on the bright image filling the screen. The darkened room was hushed, the summer air warm with bodies and anticipation.

Behind the magic lantern it was even warmer. But at last my twenty-one year old cousin Nathan had taken control of it and I could stand a little to the side. It was the final night of Father's West Dorset speaking tour and at last I could concentrate on the talk. I also kept half an eye on the audience, shadowy but just visible, their faces alert.

The image showed a young couple standing on a mountainside. The sparse landscape, dotted with trees and rocks, undulated in arid magnificence. The young man looked very proper. He wore a suit despite the apparent heat, and appeared to have been transplanted directly from the green of southern England. The woman beside him wore a beautiful Anatolian outfit: a long straight dress in red and gold over full trousers with golden braided cuffs, her dark hair half-hidden under a neat hat and veil.

'And,' declaimed Father, 'while we languished, unable to venture further, the people of the village took us in as honoured guests and in time, love blossomed among the olives. My faithful assistant Henry asked for the hand of the beautiful Cemile and her father gave his blessing.'

A collective feminine sigh rose from the audience.

'I have brought with me an embroidered hat such as Cemile wore, and her dainty shoes. And see what intricate designs the ladies painted on their hands for the wedding…'

Nathan changed the slide and the audience almost as a body leaned forward as if to trace the pattern displayed in front of them. A matron nearby muttered about heathens and painted women but her neighbours shushed her. I took the chance to survey the room. All eyes were on the screen or on Father. No-one but I noticed two men slip in through the curtained door at the back of the hall.

'Alas!' boomed Father.

The slide of the hand was replaced with a scene of devastation. Buildings were tumbled, trees uprooted. In the foreground a huge jar lay smashed, its contents spilled, and sitting on a rock, a woman cradled something in her arms.

'This land can be a cruel land. Do the dragons Ejderha and Evren yet slither through the mountains, their monstrous fiery tails causing the rocks to crack and the ground to open? Alas…' his voice trembled. 'Alas, an earthquake struck and my faithful Henry and his bride were lost.'

The audience gasped. Father had written the whole talk

11

as a tribute to his assistant Henry, making it his story from the moment they planned the expedition. It was, perhaps, the kindest thing Father had ever done.

'Yes,' said Father. 'All hands salvaged what we could of the village and rescued whomever we could find alive but Henry was gone. And yet . . . and yet . . . he is not forgotten.'

Nathan put through the final slide. 'In the land of the Black Tulips, in the wilds which once perhaps were engulfed in water, and above which Noah sailed in faithful hope of land, in the mountains where ancient dragons slither and thyme can be smelt with every footstep, Henry lies with his arms around his bride. Protecting her forever.'

Even the matron was wiping a tear.

'Thank you for listening,' said Father.

The audience rose to its feet to applaud, and I watched the two men approach someone at the end of a row. After the briefest of tussles, the third man was escorted from the room. A weight lifted from my shoulders. *Case complete.*

'Main lights on?' whispered Nathan.

I nodded and he went to turn the switches. Tomorrow we would go home, and Nathan would take over as Father's assistant. He and his widowed mother Aunt Leah would be moving into Mulberry Avenue with Father while James and I moved out. I didn't know whether to be pleased or sad.

***

'Decadence!' Ada slammed the hotel-room door behind her and wagged a finger at me. 'All this idling has made you louche, Mrs Kitty! And to think that people can see you! For shame.'

There was an hour before we needed to catch the train, and I was curled up in the window seat in Weymouth reading letters.

I blinked at Ada's attack, made a quick check of myself to ensure I was fully clothed, and then looked outside. I could see the Esplanade and beach clearly. People were walking arm in arm enjoying the summer morning. The bathing machines were pulled up on the sands ready for the off, but a few older children and youths were already paddling. However while they were all quite clear to me, it was hard to imagine any of them could have made me out even if they'd wanted to.

'I'm sorry, Ada,' I said, swinging down from the window seat and pulling out a chair for her. 'I'm not sure what I've done this time.'

'Your hair is down,' she said. 'And I saw you yesterday, looking at that shop which sells bathing costumes.' She couldn't have sounded more disapproving had she seen me swinging naked from the Jubilee Clock.

'Ada, please sit. What is it really?'

'I've been so bored,' she said, her lip quivering a tiny bit; whether from distress or fury, I couldn't tell. 'I can't wait to get home.'

'Please sit, Ada.' I rang the bell and when the maid came, ordered tea.

'It's not right, sitting having tea with you,' grumbled Ada. 'It's my job to make tea for you and go back to the kitchen.'

'Never mind. We're on holiday.'

'It's not right, being on holiday.'

Ada had refused point blank to be put up in the same hotel as Father and I for the week we'd stayed in Weymouth. From the depths of her mysterious past she had found a relation or old friend who kept a smaller establishment, and insisted on staying there. Although I had managed to prevail upon her to sit on the beach in a deck chair for a whole hour, it was only because I'd paid for its hire and she didn't like to waste money. She was so scandalised by the bare ankles on display and the distant and barely discernible 'virtually naked' bathers that I decided thereafter to only take her on excursions where people were fully clothed (except perhaps in art, which didn't apparently count). In the main, however, she had refused those too, on the grounds that she had better things to do than look at objects which needed dusting. I had the feeling the only time she'd been happy was when her relation or friend had let her help with the housework.

'Sit down, please,' I begged, waving my letters. 'I'll tell you all Connie's news.'

A soft smile replaced Ada's frown as she finally deigned to seat herself. 'Ah — and how is the blessed angel?'

'Which one? A, B or C?'

'Tut tut, Mrs Kitty.' Ada scowled again. 'Your mother and aunt didn't bring you up to be facetious.'

'I didn't think it up,' I argued. 'James did.'

Another smile. James could do no wrong in Ada's eyes. 'Gentlemen will be gentlemen. Anyway, Mr Bertie will always be Mr Bertie to me, so really there isn't an A.'

The tea had arrived and Ada insisted on pouring it as I read from Connie's letter. It didn't take long.

Bee has some teeth coming but it hasn't stopped her giggling. She is such a delight and loves the toy you bought her, though I confess I'm not sure if she prefers chewing it, shaking it or throwing it for Nanny to retrieve.

'The little darling!' interrupted Ada, with no apparent care for Nanny's feelings.

Albert is still afraid he'll break her.

'Tsk. Tell Mrs Connie to bring them both round to me and I'll set him straight.'

James came to dinner last night and seems to be missing you. (That is to say, he said the place was nice and quiet.) One suspects he's positively bored without anyone to argue with. He has refused to let me see your new apartments but promises he has taken feminine advice as to its decor. Oh, and he has a surprise for you.

Ada sniggered. I gave her a stern look but she remained unabashed.

I'm glad that your Father's lectures have gone well and your cousin Nathan is learning the ropes. I hope that Ada has enjoyed her holiday. She certainly deserved one.

'Huh.'

I can't wait to hear all about your time away, assuming Mr Maynard hasn't already an assignment lined up for you.

'Has he?' said Ada, nodding at my other letters.

'Mmm,' I replied. She narrowed her eyes, but even Ada's gimlet stare couldn't penetrate the envelope of Mr Maynard's wire, which simply said *Well done STOP Arrest*

15

successful and charges made STOP.

'It's hard for you without Mrs Connie's help,' Ada said when she realised I wouldn't vouchsafe anything.

I detected pride in her voice. Truth to tell, she respected my discretion and determination. She was one of the few people I knew who didn't say that married women shouldn't work; nor did she ever ask probing questions about the possibility of anticipated blessings. The only thing that mattered was the one thing she saw. I missed Connie's help.

'James has written too,' I told her.

She sat back. 'Ah. The Wordsmith.' It was my turn to raise my eyebrows but she didn't notice.

Dear K, do you have to come home? I am enjoying a week of good sleep without your snoring. My sister has given the apartment a once-over and chosen the furnishings. I hope you like the style of 1882. Very flouncy. If you insist on coming home, I suppose I'll have to collect you from Waterloo on Friday evening.

'That's nice,' said Ada, without irony. She thought my husband was perfect.

Went to visit ABC last night. Or rather A & C. According to Nanny I'm too boisterous for Bee in the evening and make her fractious. Utter nonsense, but at least it gave me plenty of time to talk to A & C. They have given us tickets to a masquerade ball. Hope you have been practising your dancing while you're away. You'll need a costume. I wonder if you could borrow something from the music hall. Failing that, perhaps you could go as a tulip. I, of course, shall go as a Roman Emperor.

'Shenanigans,' said Ada with relish. 'And about time too.'

CHAPTER 3
Connie

'How do I look?' I said, turning from the glass as Albert came in.

'Beautiful,' said Albert. 'Though I suspect you'll leave a trail of white everywhere you go.'

Maria had made me an exquisite white gown in the style of the eighteenth century; I required a new dress, for my figure had changed sufficiently to make all my formal dresses unwearable. Violet and Nancy had put my hair up in a suitably imposing style and powdered it white. My head felt twice as heavy as usual; but it did look striking. When I put on my white silk half-mask, a stranger gazed back at me. I wasn't sure if I liked it or not. Then again, perhaps that was part of the experience.

'I feel rather underdressed, by comparison,' said Albert, coming over to brush a little powder from my shoulder.

'It's more difficult for men,' I said. 'You look very distinguished in your white tie and tails.'

'Thank you, milady.' He stooped to kiss my cheek, staying well clear of my hair. 'I wonder what James and K will wear.'

'We'll find out soon,' I said. 'James will want to blend in, if he's covering the event for the paper.'

'I'll believe that when I see it,' said Albert. 'And K could turn up as anything.'

'True. Let's fetch them, and find out.'

***

'Good heavens,' I murmured to myself, as James and Katherine emerged from their flat. Both were wearing Greek robes which reached almost to the floor, although in Katherine's case they were drawn in at the waist by a thin gold belt. Her hair was down beneath a high crown, while James wore a laurel wreath on his head and carried a lightning bolt. The simple costumes suited them both, and for a moment I wished that Albert and I were a matching pair, too.

'Jupiter and Juno, I presume,' I said, as they approached. 'Or is it Zeus and Hera?'

'I shall answer to either,' said Katherine, looking most dignified.

'Well, you look lovely,' I said. 'I shall try not to anger you, in case you turn me into something nasty.'

'I doubt Aunt Alice would let me,' said Katherine, a trifle regretfully. 'She was most concerned that our costumes should be proper, with no chance of anything, um, showing. I daresay these sheets have no magic powers left whatsoever, she's put so many seams and darts in.'

'I'm sure my thunderbolt will do the trick,' said James,

19

brandishing it. 'Now come along, or we'll miss the fun.'

***

We drew up outside the Beaulieu Hotel a fashionable fifteen minutes late. There was nothing to indicate that anything unusual was happening, but then again, Maisie had told me that the whole affair was meant to be rather exclusive. 'Only for those in the know, dear,' she had said.

'Tredwell, would you mind waiting for ten minutes,' said Albert, opening the door and handing me out. 'If we haven't come back out looking forlorn by then, we'll see you at midnight.'

Midnight! When had I last been out at such an hour?

We entered the hotel and immediately a footman all in white, with a powdered wig, beckoned us over. 'This way, ladies and gentlemen,' he said. 'Do you have your tickets?'

He led us along a corridor, our feet silent in the thick plush carpet, and then down a short flight of steps to a pair of mirrored doors. I looked at our reflections; Albert tall and upright, myself as tall, with my piled-up white hair, James and Katherine arm in arm in their robes and headdresses, and blinked.

'You must put your masks on now,' said the footman. 'You may not enter without them.'

I fumbled in my bag and drew out my half-mask with its ribbons. Katherine and James's masks had a simple band of elastic to fasten them, and theirs were on before I had even found mine. They looked at me, blank-faced, and for some reason my hand trembled. 'Come on,' said Albert. 'I'll tie yours if you can sort mine out.'

At length we were all ready, and the doors swung open.

I waited for someone to announce us, but it seemed completely informal. Music was playing in the background, but everyone was standing in pairs and small groups, talking and laughing.

And what a collection they were! There must have been half a dozen candles in the room, a bevy of angels, and a flock of birds, as well as a host of women in white muslin gowns. There were Pierrots, and classically-draped statues, and a man in a suit made of paper. The room itself had arrangements of white flowers standing on white plinths, with gauzy hangings all round, and chairs with white covers ringed the room. White lights twinkled everywhere.

'Do you think this is what heaven is like?' I asked Katherine.

'Heaven might be a little less busy,' she replied, with a broad smile. 'But it is very nice.'

'Connie!' said Maisie's voice, and a woman wearing a feather-trimmed dress and a matching, close-fitting cap approached. 'It is Connie, isn't it?'

'It is,' I replied, embracing her carefully.

'I feel as if I should curtsey to you.' She laughed. 'Although I do think I make rather a fine swan.'

A man in a matching feather-trimmed suit approached, holding two glasses of champagne. 'There you are!' he said. 'I thought you were staying by the pillar. I've had enough trouble finding a drink without you disappearing.'

'Sorry, Archie,' said Maisie, relieving him of a glass. 'Everyone, this is Archie Bellairs. Archie, this motley crew are Connie and Albert Lamont, and…' She looked at me for help.

'Allow me to introduce Katherine and James King,' I said. 'Katherine, James, may I introduce Maisie Frobisher.'

'Delighted,' said James, bowing over her hand and managing to keep his wreath on.

'James King…' I heard the frown in Archie Bellairs's voice. 'Now how do I know that name?'

'I write for the newspapers,' said James. 'You may have read me in the *Times*.'

'Oh, so you're here on a job!' exclaimed Archie. 'Society column, eh?'

'Who knows,' said James, 'I might even mention you.' He exchanged a hint of a grin with Katherine. She rolled her eyes ever so slightly.

Archie blinked. 'Oh — of course — you are one of the Oxfordshire Kings, aren't you?'

'Not quite royalty yet,' said James.

Archie chuckled and clapped James on the shoulder as if they were old friends. 'Now then, old chap…'

Katherine tucked her arm in mine and steered me away. 'What an idiot that man is,' she chuckled. 'I've a good mind to tell James to write something scathing about snobs in his article.'

'It would be more fun to summon your powers and turn him into a real swan,' I said.

'Yes.' Katherine grinned. 'A mute one.'

***

We rejoined the group as a slim, fair-haired figure in white tie and tails jumped on the dais at the front of the room. 'Good evening, ladies and gentlemen!' he called.

I leaned towards Albert. 'Is that Toby Langlands?'

'Must be,' he replied.

'Welcome to our masked ball! It's wonderful to see so many of you here, supporting the All Hallows Orphanage. Supper will be served at ten, but first and foremost this is a ball, so we must have dancing!' Toby Langlands grinned. 'You will note that there are no dance cards. First come, first served!'

'Don't leave me,' I muttered to Albert.

'Don't be silly, Connie,' he replied, squeezing my hand. 'Who else would put up with my dancing?'

'I claim the first dance,' said James, taking Katherine's hand. 'Although I'm not sure what we'll dance to. We're several musicians short of a ball.'

'Good luck, everyone!' called Toby Langlands. He jumped down and was lost in the crowd.

A buzz of conversation followed as waiters circulated with trays of drinks, and then the room fell silent as four black-haired, olive-skinned men, also in white tie and tails, ascended the dais. Two held guitars, while one had a tambourine. The last man approached the upright piano at the back of the dais, rolling it on its castors so that it half-faced the audience, while the guitar players fetched chairs and took a seat. Then he came forward.

'Good evening,' he said, his English heavily accented. 'We play for you.'

As if by magic the crowd resolved itself into little islands of paired men and women.

'I have a distinct feeling that they won't be starting with Sir Roger de Coverley,' said James, turning to face

Katherine.

What followed was like nothing I had heard at a ball before. The music was slow, syncopated, and the tambourine player sang a winding melody in words I could not understand.

'I don't know what to do!' I hissed at Albert. 'What are you laughing at?'

'Look around you,' he replied. 'No one knows what to do!'

He was right. People were swaying to the music, their feet tapping, but the room was almost still.

One of the guitarists stood up, smiling broadly, and propped his guitar against the chair, even as the music continued. He walked to the front of the stage and surveyed us, then descended the steps. He was a short, slight man, and his path was towards Katherine. 'May I 'ave this dance?' he asked, bowing.

Katherine looked at James, eyebrows raised, then nodded.

'We show them tango.' He led Katherine up the steps, and put his other hand on her waist, keeping plenty of distance between them. 'So.' He moved with the rhythms of the music, almost at a walk, piloting Katherine now forward, now back, using the full width of the dais, twisting, turning, lunging. It seemed like a mix of a waltz, and a polka, and something I had never seen — something thrilling. 'Slow, slow, quick, quick, slow,' he said. 'The music tell you what to do.' He released Katherine, who was rather flushed, and they bowed to each other before he returned to his guitar.

'May I?' said Albert, and put his arm around my waist, drawing me somewhat closer than the demonstrated distance.

I looked up at him. 'Of course.'

***

Perhaps it was the unaccustomed exercise, or the effort of half-leading Albert, or the heat of the room, but I was tired after four dances, and retired to the edge of the room while Albert went in search of drinks. Katherine joined me, bright-eyed and extremely pleased with herself.

'You've cheered up, then,' I said, smiling.

'It's very exciting, isn't it?' Her cheeks were pink. 'And such fun! I hope we get to dance like this again.' She looked round the room at the weaving mass of dancers. 'I shall tell Mr Templeton that he was completely wrong.'

'What do you mean?'

'Oh, didn't I say? I meant to.' Her eyes twinkled. 'I dropped in to the Merrymakers to see if they had any costumes I could borrow, and when I mentioned what it was for, Mr T warned me off. Said he'd been approached by someone to hire a few of his girls for a — what did he say? Posing.'

'Like a tableau?'

'I think so. The man was a bit vague about what it would entail, so Mr T packed him off, especially as he said the fee was far too high for anything legitimate.' Katherine giggled. 'I'm sure I don't know what he meant.'

'Are you enjoying the ball, Mrs Lamont?' Toby Langlands had appeared out of nowhere.

I smiled. 'Very much. And do call me Connie.'

'Could I persuade you to a dance? I promise to be gentle,' he added, when he saw me hesitate.

I looked for Albert, but couldn't see him in the packed room. 'Yes, of course.'

Toby was a good dancer — I hadn't expected him to be a bad one, but he led me expertly, holding me at a respectable distance, and I glided smoothly round the room in his arms. 'You are so clever,' I murmured, 'organising all this.'

Toby laughed and pivoted me round. 'Oh, it isn't just me, not at all. I'm front of house. I know people, and they know me.'

I studied him as we crossed the room. He was much the same as the first time we had met, at Maisie's house — boyish and charming — but there was something else; a slight hardness about the corners of his mouth. I wondered how difficult things were for him. Hopefully James would write a sparkling account of the evening.

Toby met my eyes, and I tried to think of a response. 'Have you any more surprises in store?' I asked.

'Oh yes.' He laughed.

'My friend was just saying that someone from here wanted to borrow some music hall performers.' I grinned. 'Was that you?'

His smile was gone in an instant, and his face was as blank as his mask. 'As I said, I'm front of house only.'

'Now then, what's all this?' Albert was beside us, a drink in each hand. 'Sneaking off with my wife, Langlands?'

'Keeping her entertained, Lamont,' Toby replied, a

trifle stiffly, and stepped aside. 'If you'll excuse me.'

Albert gave me one of the glasses. 'What's upset him?' he asked in an undertone, as we walked back to the chairs, where James and Katherine were chatting happily like deities at play.

'I'm not sure,' I said, taking a seat and sipping my drink. 'He probably wants to make sure everything's running smoothly. I heard Archie Bellairs holding forth about the waiters earlier.'

Albert snorted. 'That's more about him than the waiters, in my opinion.'

We had just taken to the floor again when a shot rang out. Several ladies screamed, and one man threw himself to the ground.

The doors burst open, and in rushed a group of black-cloaked, masked men in wide-brimmed hats, each brandishing . . . a child's hobby-horse.

'We are the Masquerade Mob!' they shouted, as one. 'We are highwaymen who rob from the rich to give to charity! Stand and deliver!'

The room filled with laughter and exclamation as the highwaymen approached different groups, soliciting donations for their horses' nosebags. I saw banknotes and sovereigns disappearing into the bags, along with some pieces of jewellery. Albert put a note into the bag, but I had nothing to give except a pair of earrings with paste stones. 'They aren't real, I'm afraid,' I said, as I unscrewed them. 'But perhaps you can get a little money for them.'

'I'm sure we can, ma'am,' said the highwayman, bowing. 'Thank you very much.' And he kissed my hand before proceeding to his next victim.

As we grew more practised at dancing the band played faster, and we enjoyed ourselves so much that it was a shame to stop for supper; but the exquisite morsels provided — the little pastries, the flavoured ices — were perfectly refreshing, and the end of the evening seemed to arrive in a flash.

'I feel like Cinderella,' I sighed, as the hands of the huge wall clock sped towards twelve.

'Let's hope our coach hasn't turned into a pumpkin,' said Albert. 'It's a long walk home from here.'

As the band finished their number Toby Langlands sprang onto the stage. 'Please show your appreciation for our band!' he called, and led the hearty applause.

Behind me I could hear a woman's voice. 'Excuse me . . . excuse me...' It sounded familiar, somehow, and I turned to try and make out who it was — but all I could see was a slim brown-haired figure in a sleeveless shift swaying through the crowd. She looked in my direction once, but her mask covered her face completely. Perhaps she was Cinderella, hurrying to her carriage.

'I must say goodbye to Maisie, and thank her for inviting us,' I said. 'It's been such a lovely evening.' Now I came to think of it, I hadn't seen Maisie for at least an hour — and her swan costume was distinctive. 'Where can she be?'

I got my answer a few minutes later, when the crowds began to thin. Maisie stalked over looking anything but serene. 'You haven't seen Archie, have you?' she snapped. 'He's vanished, and I didn't see him leave.'

I shook my head, as did the others. 'I don't think I've seen him since before supper.'

'Which I missed, hunting for him.' Maisie's laugh was brittle. 'Oh well, he can walk home then. Last time I take him anywhere.' She hurried to the exit, feathers wafting.

'Maybe he died of embarrassment at his outfit,' murmured James. 'Or flew away.'

'Unless Katherine rediscovered her powers,' I replied.

I think we were all tired on the journey home, for we were certainly quieter than usual. I leaned on Albert's shoulder, careless of my hair — I did not want to think how long I might be up, with Violet, getting the powder and pomade out.

Once we had dropped Jupiter and Juno off, Albert's arm snaked round my shoulders. 'Did you enjoy it, Connie?'

'I loved it.' I snuggled down. 'Did you?'

He laughed. 'It was fun. Langlands did a good job, I thought. I shall have to see when his next event is.' He yawned widely. 'I'll sleep like a baby tonight.'

And that was when I realised I had not thought of Bee all evening.

CHAPTER 4
Katherine

'Did you really go to the music-hall to borrow a costume?' asked Connie, as we sat in the sunny park outside my new home in Bayswater's Joyce Square.

I nearly said yes but Connie looked too fidgety to tease, not used to being a whole mile and a half from Bee without dancing to distract her.

'No, not really. I doubt they have anything in white,' I said. 'But I thought they might have some ideas and besides, I like to pop in from time to time. It's good to keep in touch.'

'And you and James weren't wearing bedsheets either, were you?'

'Hardly.' It always baffled me how little someone so well-dressed knew about fabric. 'Anyway, Aunt Alice would never waste good bed linen on frivolity.'

'Was she very disapproving?'

'Pretended to be.' I grinned, thinking of Aunt Alice's

face, torn between pride at being asked to make costumes when I could have gone to Maria, anxiety in case she made a mistake, concern about propriety, and sharing in my excitement. 'I think she was pleased for me. She was just worried that the crowd might be a little giddy, and more importantly that James's bare legs would show. He said he would wear a bathing suit underneath and she looked more horrified than if he'd said he would simply wear his underwear.'

Connie chuckled, but looked a little horrified herself.

'Don't worry, Connie,' I clarified. 'He said it was a bit bulky with trousers and socks but didn't think hairy legs would look quite right with dancing shoes.'

'But they were wonderful, weren't they?' said Connie. 'The costumes I mean, not James's legs. And the ball was marvellous! Did you enjoy it?'

'Of course I did! It was the loveliest thing I've done for ages.'

The park in Joyce Square was a very small piece of greenery, with a railing around it, faced on three sides by tall houses and on the fourth by a road. Compared to the park near my old home in Fulham, it was a mere handkerchief of green. Compared to Hyde Park and Regent's Park a short walk away, it was a postage stamp. But all the same it was pleasant. James had bought the lease for the upper two floors and attic of number twelve, one of the houses which faced south onto the park. The house was well built and the old lady on the ground floor was quiet and delightful, but it didn't quite feel like home yet.

Connie followed my gaze and her smile dropped. 'Oh Katherine, I'm sorry we didn't get everything ready for you before you returned from Dorset.'

I wondered what she meant. Regardless of what they'd said in their letters, James and Connie had arranged the redecorating between them. The apartment was up to the minute and beautiful. Connie had a wonderful eye when not being criticised by her mother.

'But you did,' I said. 'It's lovely.'

'But we didn't find you a very good maid.'

'Susan is doing perfectly well. She just can't cook anything more complicated than soup and sandwiches. It feels quite decadent eating out every evening, and James knows out of the way, inexpensive places with foreign food I've never heard of.'

In truth I was getting a little tired of eating out and food I'd never heard of, but there was no point in complaining. We'd find a cook at some point.

Connie's gaze followed a young nanny pushing a perambulator round the park. An insistent wail came from within. Connie's hands clenched.

'Bee is perfectly fine,' I said. 'She has Nanny to care for her. It won't do her an ounce of harm if you come outside for a change.'

I had no idea whether what I said was true or not, but one could hardly call Bee neglected, and besides she seemed to spend a lot of her time asleep. I cast my mind back to the age of nine when my sister Margaret had been born. Maybe it was because Mother's death meant she was brought up by hired nurses and Aunt Alice, or maybe it was just the way she was, but Margaret had been the most demanding, sleepless baby anyone had ever known. 'Wilful,' declared hired nurse number three as she walked out. 'Naughty. If I stay a moment longer, I shall lose my sanity.' If I ever had a baby of my own I hoped it would be somewhere between Bee and Margaret in temperament; either extreme would make me lose *my* sanity.

'Never mind,' said Connie, looking at her watch and rising. 'We ought to be going. Mina will be waiting for us.'

I laughed. 'We have plenty of time. However did you manage not to be early on Saturday evening?'

'Oh you know,' said Connie. 'Albert is like a kind of brake. Katherine, may I ask . . . how is your work? Can you talk about it?'

'Of course I can,' I said, standing and hooking my arm through hers as we walked to the tea-shop. 'You are still on Mr Maynard's books ready for when . . . if you want to return. It's quite ad hoc now. Exciting. One never knows what's going to turn up next.'

'You seem to have been doing well enough without me.'

I tried to think of a reply that wouldn't make her think I didn't miss her help, or wouldn't put her under pressure when she wasn't ready to return, or indeed, didn't want to.

'When you're ready to join me again, if you want to, I'll buy you buns for a whole week,' I said, in the end. 'And for as long as you don't, you have to be prepared to meet me for lunch in down-at-heel restaurants on demand. In either case, you can bring Bee if you like. She could be "cover".'

'Agreed,' said Connie. She looked thoughtful, and I wondered what was going through her mind. 'Now tell me what you were up to in Weymouth. You weren't just organising magic lantern shows, I'm sure of it.'

'Well...'

***

At the tea-shop Mina enquired about Dorset and chuckled at my description of Ada on the beach, sitting under a black umbrella to protect her from the blazing sun, muttering as yet another otherwise respectable matron somehow removed her stockings discreetly to stand at the edge of the water in bare feet. But her laughter was soon replaced by a faint air of disquiet. She seemed subdued.

Connie and I exchanged glances. 'Is Dr Farquhar well?'

'Oh yes,' said Mina. I was pleased to see a tiny sparkle in her eye and a small smile as she thought of him. 'He is giving a lecture tour of his own shortly and has asked me to help with organising it. I shall accompany him on his first London engagement next week. It is quite late in the evening, so we shall have to dine out first. You may like to come. To the lecture that is, I'm sure you have better things to do than dine with two dull middle-aged people. He'll be speaking on new ideas about disturbances of the mind.' She grew thoughtful again. 'He believes sufferers should not be afraid to own up to their condition, should not be scared to seek help. But it is very hard. People can be so judgmental and yet there is so much despair which perhaps could be alleviated...' Her face was troubled.

'Mina . . . you can talk to us,' I said. 'We shared our deepest fears and anxieties last year. Nothing could shock us and you know we won't judge.'

'Oh, it's not me,' she said. 'It's just . . . I don't want to break a confidence.'

'You're not under the Hippocratic oath,' said Connie. 'And we all signed the Official Secrets Act. We'll never share anything you tell us, and you need to tell someone. If not us, maybe Dr Farquhar.'

'Oh I couldn't bother him, it's all speculation, I'm sure. He is a person who likes facts and usually so am I, but…' Mina took a deep breath. 'As you know, I do a lot of listening. I hear a lot of worrying over next to nothing and I'm sure it's been the same since ancient times, and will be the same in the year two thousand.' Her laugh was brittle. 'But in this last week three young people have come to see me in absolute despair. Well-off young men with everything to live for, and yet…'

Connie put her hand over Mina's. 'Go on, don't worry.'

Mina swallowed and glanced round the tearoom. 'I am afraid they might do themselves harm. I did my best, of course, but….' She shook herself. 'Perhaps it's the heat. Or more likely my imagination. Thank you for listening. Now, Connie, cheer us up before Katherine has to leave us to see Mr Maynard. Tell me all the news about Bee. Have you any photographs?'

***

'Well done,' said Mr Maynard, sliding my report into a large envelope and sealing it with wax. 'Very well done indeed. That elusive gentleman posed a great risk to security and I was quite unsure how we would corner him.'

'Thank you, sir.'

Mr Maynard steepled his fingers, perusing me. I no longer had the large room on the upper floor since I worked alone, and only had to attend the Department to obtain my assignments. I had been given a typewriter, James had taught me shorthand, and I used a small back room in Joyce Square as an office.

'Did no-one in your family notice your activities?'

I chuckled. Clearly I should introduce Mr Maynard to Father. 'No, sir. My father is very much absorbed in his work and tends not to pay a great deal of attention to anything else. And my cousin was learning how to take over from me as Father's assistant.'

'Ah yes, Nathan Lawrenson, Esquire, son of the estimable Leah Lawrenson, née Demeray, and Hammond Lawrenson, deceased.'

'Yes, sir.'

'Deceased very impecuniously.'

I raised my eyebrows.

'You know I have to make these enquiries, Mrs King.'

'Yes, sir. I am sure you found no impropriety in the Lawrenson household. It was very strict. My uncle disapproved of Father and insisted they had nothing to do with us. I am sure he's turning in his grave thinking of Aunt Leah and Nathan under Father's roof.'

Mr Maynard let out a sigh. 'Well, he should have been more careful in his investments so that he could leave more than debt. Still, I found nothing else untoward. What about the inestimable Ada? I can't imagine she was oblivious to your investigations.'

'I think she was too affronted by being on holiday and

36

idle, sir.'

'Good, good. Well, I have nothing at present for you, so I hope you won't be affronted by idleness but make the most of it. The sun is shining, the air is as clear as it ever gets in London, the Thames is at least more fragrant than it was a few years ago, and I daresay your father is seeking out new adventures.'

I blinked. I wondered why the man had asked us to investigate psychics when he appeared to be one himself. 'Why yes, sir, he is on a hunt for dinosaurs.'

'How intriguing. Now then,' Mr Maynard stood and ushered me to the door. 'I shall be in touch as soon as I have another assignment and in the meantime, as ever, if Mrs Lamont wishes to rejoin the fold, I hope she knows she is very welcome. I miss her typing and would like to see what she makes of shorthand.' He held the door open and followed me through into the cool, stark foyer where he shook my hand.

A very smart gentleman was standing close by, talking to a group of Mr Maynard's counterparts. From the quality of his clothes and haughtiness of his demeanour, I doubted he was a civil servant, even a very senior one. He might be a member of parliament with ministerial responsibility, although he looked more like nobility than a commoner. He was probably there to complain about something and demand action.

Mr Maynard and I bowed farewell to each other, then as I passed through the double doors I heard a gasp. 'Who is that woman with the red hair?' But when I turned to see who had spoken, the group of men had moved away.

CHAPTER 5
Connie

'Who's your letter from?'

Albert looked reprovingly over the top of the paper he was engrossed in. 'Connie, such grammar!' Then he grinned and held it out to me. 'It's from Langlands.'

My dear Lamont,

Just a few lines to thank you for coming on Saturday — and more particularly for getting your friend to write it up in the Times. I read King's column regularly, and I know it isn't at all his usual sort of thing, so I appreciate the favour all the more, even under a pseudonym.

I hope you enjoyed the ball as much as I did, and that you and your friends will accept further invitations. Our next event will be in August, and I plan to make it bigger and better than the first. We raised a substantial amount for the All Hallows Orphanage thanks to the generous donations of people such as yourself. It's a pleasure to know that we can have fun and do good at the same time.

Yours,

Toby Langlands

'That's nice,' I said, passing it back. 'Especially since it means we're invited to another event. I wonder what it will be?'

Albert scrutinised me, a smile on his face. 'You look so excited, Connie.'

'I am,' I said. 'Another evening out to look forward to, and Katherine has a new assignment.'

'Does she?'

'Mr Maynard wired to say he would call on her at nine today.' Now it was my turn to study Albert. 'If it's something I could help with…'

'You want to go back?' I couldn't quite read Albert's expression.

'I'm not sure,' I said. 'I couldn't leave Bee for a whole day. But perhaps here and there.'

Albert's face relaxed from what I now realised had been an assumed composure. 'That's all right then. I would like to see you sometimes, you know. Other than at mealtimes. Just — stay out of trouble.'

I leaned over and kissed him. 'Of course I shall.'

***

I was up in the nursery when I heard the doorbell. I glanced at the clock on the mantel — a quarter past ten. Could it be Katherine? It seemed too early, but then who else would call at this time? I listened, but whoever it was spoke low.

'I can take Miss Bee,' said Nanny, hovering nearby.

I kissed Bee's forehead and transferred her carefully over. 'I'll be back soon, poppet.' I heard Nancy's footsteps. The proper thing to do would be to wait until she entered; but I was too impatient for propriety. I opened the nursery door and mouthed 'Who is it?'

'It's Mrs King, ma'am,' Nancy replied. I checked that my clothes were in order, then hurried downstairs.

Katherine was standing in the hall, neat as ever in her green day-dress, but with her veil pulled down. 'Katherine! What did he say? Come up to my boudoir, you can tell me about it there.'

Katherine didn't move. And now I thought of it, Nancy had looked rather serious when she came upstairs. I reached for her hands. 'What is it? Has something happened? What's wrong?'

'I'll tell you upstairs,' she muttered. She did not speak again till we were safely shut away. She raised her veil at last, and it was obvious that, as much as Katherine hated tears, she had been crying.

'It wasn't an assignment,' she said, and every word seemed to wound her as it came out. 'Mr Maynard called at the house because I can't go to the Department any more. I've been dismissed.'

***

An age passed before I could find words. 'But why? How?'

Katherine wiped the last sign of tears away. 'Immoral behaviour, apparently.' She shrugged. 'Somehow it came to the attention of Lord Marchmont that I attended the

40

masked ball on Saturday. He's obviously read one of the more lurid accounts in the papers — *his* papers, no doubt — and assumed the worst.'

'But why should it matter to him?' I put an arm around Katherine, who was shaking like a leaf.

'He's a minister. He has a lot of influence in Parliament. He could put pressure on the Treasury to reduce the Department's budget...' Katherine hiccupped. 'He's strongly against any suspicion of impropriety, and to him dancing the tango in a floor-length robe, even in my own time, is gross misconduct.'

'How does he know? He wasn't there! And nothing happened!'

'I know that.' Katherine's words were bitter as black coffee. 'You know that. I suspect Mr Maynard knows it too. But it doesn't matter. If dismissing me keeps Lord Marchmont happy, that's what they have to do.' She swallowed, painfully. 'I asked if I could continue to work in secret, unpaid perhaps, but —' She shook her head. 'Mr Maynard's been severely reprimanded for employing me at all. He said he only just retained his own position.'

'What a mess,' I said. 'What a complete, utter, unfair mess.'

'At least I wasn't doing it for the money any more,' said Katherine, with a small pained smile. 'I can behave like a proper lady at last. A lady with nothing to do but lunch and attend soirées.'

'I'm so sorry,' I said, giving her a squeeze which seemed entirely inadequate. 'I know what it meant to you.'

'Past tense already.' Katherine sighed. 'That's why I

came to you. I knew you'd understand. James is at work, and he'll be furious when he hears, but — there's nothing he can do. Journalism's a small world, and people like Lord Marchmont hold all the cards. Except he probably doesn't approve of that, either.'

***

Over the next fortnight I spent more time with Katherine than I had since our days at the music hall. We had lunch together, of course, and walked in the park with Bee, and I took her to call on Maisie Frobisher, whose spirits were quite restored.

'Did you ever track down Mr Bellairs?' I asked, reaching for a finger sandwich.

Maisie looked blank for a moment, then laughed. 'Oh, Archie! Mr Bellairs, indeed.' She wrinkled her nose scornfully. 'He called to apologise the next day. Apparently he "came over dizzy" and decided to go home.' She snorted. 'I can't abide a man who isn't able to hold his drink.'

'Oh Maisie, that's rather harsh,' I said. Katherine said nothing, but her green eyes were thoughtful.

'Well, really,' said Maisie, taking an iced fondant. 'I expect a man to look after *me*, not the other way around.' She bit into the fondant decisively, as if it were Archie Bellairs.

'Do you think he really *was* taken ill?' Katherine asked me in the carriage.

I shrugged. 'It's possible. Maybe the tango had a bad effect on him. I don't know him well enough to say.' That in itself was strange — Maisie and I had moved in similar

42

social circles all our lives. But then, I had been so busy with other matters in the last few years that a hundred men could have come and gone from my social circle and I would not have noticed.

***

That thought would haunt me the very next morning. Johnson had brought in the post at breakfast; nothing for me, but two or three letters for Albert. I was busy with my boiled egg when a half-strangled cry from across the table made me look up.

Albert was staring at a black-edged card as if it were a poisonous snake, and his face had lost all its colour.

My spoon clattered on the plate and I rushed to him. 'Albert, what is it?' I cried, putting my arms round him.

'Who is it, you mean.' He laughed, and it was a horrible sound. 'I can't believe it.' He pressed the card into my hand.

Mr and Mrs Albert Lamont are respectfully requested to attend the funeral of Tobias Langlands, Esq —

'What? No!' I almost dropped the card.

— at St Peter's Church, on Thursday 17th August, at two o'clock.

'But — but he was perfectly well! I danced with him a fortnight ago!'

'I know.' Albert ran his hands through his hair. 'I don't understand.' He stood up and rang the bell. 'Johnson, can you bring me any back copies of the *Times* which are still in the house, please.'

Johnson's eyes opened wide as he saw the card on the table. 'Yes, sir. Certainly, sir.'

He returned a few minutes later with one crumpled newspaper. 'I'm sorry, sir, yesterday's is all that's left. The rest has gone for boot-cleaning or been thrown out.'

'Thank you.' Albert riffled through the paper once the footman had gone. 'I don't even know where to look,' he muttered. 'I've never needed to know before.' Eventually he found the right page, ran a finger down the columns, and shook his head, closing the paper and refolding it. 'Whatever it was, I hope he didn't suffer.' He stood, pushing his chair back. 'I'm sorry, Connie, I need to be alone.'

***

The funeral was well-attended, mostly, it seemed, by family friends and men who had known Toby at school. 'It's like sitting in morning prayers ten years on,' Albert muttered, eyeing the rows of bowed heads. The coffin stood at the front of the church, closed and crowned with white and purple flowers. It held a horrible fascination for me. I did not want to look at it, yet I had to — but it felt wrong.

The service began. I had never attended a funeral before, and was not sure what to expect; but it turned out to be much the same as any other church service. In the front pew I saw a man with iron-grey hair and an almost unnaturally straight back — that must be Toby's father, Sir Peter Langlands — and a row of young men who were, presumably, Toby's elder brothers. *The youngest brother of five*, I thought, recalling my mother's copy of *Debrett's Peerage*. I couldn't see any women in the front pew. Perhaps his mother and sister — sisters? — had remained at home, unable to face the ordeal.

I tried to focus on what the priest was saying, but his voice was so soothing and monotonous that the words flowed past, around the coffin in which lay Toby Langlands, who had been so full of life the last time I saw him —

'Tobias Langlands, the unhappy victim of a tragic accident…' the priest intoned.

The hairs on the back of my neck stood up. What on earth had happened? But the priest gave no clue, as he instructed us to bow our heads in prayer.

A hymn followed, and then it was time to process past the coffin, the closed coffin which now I could not look at. Albert held my arm securely. 'Are you all right, Connie?' he asked, his face pale and set.

I could only nod. I couldn't meet his eyes in case he saw my thoughts. Now was not the time, or the place. It was a relief to walk into the open air, even though I knew that soon Toby Langlands' coffin would follow us down the path to its final resting place.

The priest hurried towards us, followed at a steadier pace by the coffin, borne by Toby's brothers and two undertakers, with Toby's father walking alongside. More words were said at the graveside. The priest handed Sir Peter a small trowel to sprinkle earth on the coffin, and then laid more words on top of that. Out of the corner of my eye I saw the gravediggers in a quiet corner, waiting to finish their work. A final prayer, and it was over. The wind sighed in the trees. It felt as if it should have been a winter day, but it was still bright summer, and the sunlight and green leaves jarred painfully with the sight before us.

'I must go and pay my respects to Sir Peter,' said Albert. 'Will you come too, Connie?'

'Of course,' I said. The alternative was to stand alone with my uncomfortable thoughts.

Sir Peter was standing at the foot of the grave while his sons shook hands with departing guests. He looked the sort of man who would grip Albert's offered hand firmly, but he barely pressed it. 'I am so sorry, Sir Peter,' said Albert.

'So am I,' said Toby's father, his gaze turned inward. Then he looked up at Albert. 'Lamont, isn't it? The youngest?'

'That's right, sir. I was at school with William.'

'That's it.' His expression softened a little. 'Toby spoke well of you. Said you'd helped him out of a,' — he winced — 'a hole a couple of times. Financially.'

'It was nothing,' said Albert.

'I seem to remember something about you and tulips in the paper, a few years back. Black tulips.' He managed a grim smile. 'A subject dear to my family's heart.'

'Oh, that was blown out of all proportion,' said Albert. 'You know what the papers are like.'

'I do,' said Sir Peter. 'I wonder if you would do me the favour of coming back to the house.'

***

'It's probably nothing,' said Albert, as the carriage rattled towards Lowndes Square. 'He probably wants to reminisce about happier times, and I don't blame him. What a terrible thing to happen.' But the arm he had put

46

around me was trembling.

I looked up at him. 'We'll find out soon.'

He nodded, and his blue eyes were clouded.

Lowndes Square was leafy and pleasant, a smart lawn surrounded by mature trees, and bordered by tall brown-brick townhouses. The Langlands' house was perfectly respectable, but perhaps a little barer than the other houses in the row; there were no window-boxes bright with geraniums, no vases or statues on the windowsills. The parlour in which we waited for Sir Peter was the same; irreproachable, clean, but spare in its decoration.

'I apologise for keeping you waiting,' said Sir Peter. 'Please, come through to my study. I have ordered tea.'

Curiouser and curiouser, I thought, as we followed Sir Peter to a small, cosy room tucked away at the back of the house. He offered us the two leather armchairs, comfortable but worn, and sat behind the desk, where a tea-tray waited.

'Shall I pour?' I asked.

'That would be very kind, Mrs Lamont,' said Sir Peter. 'I believe you also knew Toby.'

'I did,' I said, concentrating on holding the teapot steady.

'He said you were involved in the matter of the tulips, too.'

'More than I was, in fact,' said Albert. 'My cousin Katherine was part of it as well.'

Sir Peter watched me pour tea into the third cup, and add milk. 'Then I assume you can keep a secret.'

Albert and I looked at each other. 'Yes,' we said.

Sir Peter opened his desk drawer, drew out a sheet of cream-coloured paper, and placed it on the green leather.

'Go on,' he said. 'Read it.'

I unfolded the sheet. The writing was Toby's.

I am in a hole, and this is the only way out.

You will find me inside the boatman's hut at Raymond Park.

I am so sorry.

I laid the note gently on the desk.

'Our butler gave this to me when I returned from a dinner engagement,' said Sir Peter. 'It had come in the evening post. I made an excuse to my wife, and took William with me.' He paused, as if to gather what remaining strength he had. 'We found Toby. He had shot himself through the heart. We brought him home. I said it was an accident, must have been. I couldn't bear the thought of Toby being buried away from the family, in unconsecrated ground. We have had enough scandal over the years.' His head was low, and I could see how much even this simple admission had cost him.

'Why are you telling us this, sir?' asked Albert, quietly.

'Toby was a good boy,' said Sir Peter. 'He knew right from wrong. He wouldn't have hurt a fly. I can't bring him back, but I can find out who brought him to this, and bring them to justice.' He drew the letter towards him, and locked it in the desk. 'The police aren't an option,' he said. 'The shock and the shame of it would finish us. But you —' His glance did not waver. 'You understand how it is. You can be discreet. I can trust you.'

Albert looked at me. 'What do you think, Connie?'

'Please,' said Sir Peter. 'There is no one else to ask. You are my only hope.'

I swallowed. 'We can try.' Sir Peter held out his hand, and first I, then Albert shook it. 'We will try.'

CHAPTER 6
Katherine

It was Saturday afternoon. I sat staring at what I'd typed, on the machine Mr Maynard had said I need not return.

'There's people, mum,' said Susan, stepping in to the room.

'People?'

'Well there's a lady, there's a woman and there's a baby. Shall I show them into the sitting room or what, mum?'

'They're early. Yes, please do, and then bring us some tea.' I rose and made my way to the floor below, dragging my thoughts into the here and now. Something elusive nagged at my mind but it would have to wait. Perhaps it would come more easily if I had a distraction.

Bee was certainly that. I had only seen her a few days before, when the most exciting thing she could do was roll over, and all of a sudden there she was, sitting on my rug like a tiny empress, chewing her rattle. At the sight of me she threw the rattle across the floor, waved her little arms as if she was trying to fly and then grinned. Nanny stooped for the rattle and handed it back, and Bee threw it again and giggled.

I kissed Connie on the cheek and then swooped to lift Bee up in the air.

'My goodness, Connie,' I said. 'Are you feeding her bricks?'

'I blame the way Mrs Jones makes porridge,' said Connie. 'She is clever though, isn't she?'

'Mrs Jones?'

'No, silly. Bee. Mother says she might injure her spine by sitting up too soon. Nanny thinks she's simply ahead and obviously very intelligent. She didn't call Mother a fool, but it was written all over her face.' Connie looked quite gratified. She put her hands out and I put Bee into her lap. Bee accepted a proffered doll and started chewing its head.

Susan returned with the tea-tray and after a moment's hesitation put it on a table some distance from anyone, her face pensive and hopeful.

'Would you like to hold her?' said Connie.

'Yes please, mum!'

'Come and sit here next to Nanny. Here you are.' Connie handed Bee over and gestured for me to follow her to the window.

We looked down onto the little park and I rested my forehead against the cool glass. I had been so wrapped up in my thoughts, I hadn't realised what a nice day it was.

'Thank you for coming, Connie. You should be out with Albert somewhere.'

'Nonsense. I needed a challenge and I can tell you that finding a cab to manage two women, a baby and the perambulator is very invigorating.'

'The perambulator?'

'Well she's a bit of a weight now, as you can tell. I said we could carry her wrapped in a shawl, but Nanny nearly went purple at the thought of a refined baby being carried like a dock-worker's child.'

We both turned to look at the refined baby. She threw the dribble-covered doll on the floor and waved her arms until Nanny gave her the rattle. A lunatic tinkling of bells filled the room.

'I am so sorry I gave Bee a noisy toy,' I said. 'It must drive you frantic.'

'Well, not so much me, I suppose.' Connie sighed. I could imagine that secretly she longed to be carrying Bee in a shawl close to her heart rather than spending most of her time away from her. I gave her a small hug.

'I hope the funeral wasn't too awful,' I said. 'Sir Peter must be terribly distressed. A child shouldn't die before its parent.'

'That's partly why I'm here,' said Connie, her voice dropped to a whisper. 'I was engaged with Mother and Jemima all day yesterday and it wasn't something I could write down. I can't speak where there is any risk I can be overheard.' She raised her voice. 'I thought perhaps we could go for a walk. We are so close to Hyde Park and Bee will love to see the ducks.'

***

'I see,' I said, when Connie explained what Sir Peter

52

had told them. 'That's so terribly sad.'

Connie and I were walking arm in arm under our parasols, well out of earshot of anyone.

'And you understand why I couldn't write?' said Connie. I could feel her tension.

'Yes of course. How utterly terrible. Toby just didn't seem the sort to…'

'No, he didn't, did he?'

I thought of the words I'd been typing earlier. Thoughts really, not proper sentences.

'I wouldn't like you to think I was keeping secrets,' Connie burst out.

'I wanted to speak to you about Toby too. I had a letter from someone I knew at school. I barely recall her, but she had remembered me and tracked me down.'

Connie stopped walking and stared. 'But what…'

'She was at the ball. I wouldn't have recognised her even without a mask, but she recognised me because of my hair,' I tried to smile. 'Please remind me to wear a wig or powder at the next one.'

'If there is a next one…' Connie gave me a sharp look. 'Would you attend, after what happened?'

'Definitely. Might as well be hanged for a sheep as a lamb.'

'Good, but take it from me, don't use powder. All that aside, what has this lady to do with Toby?'

'She knew him. She is distraught.'

Connie shook her head. 'There was no young woman at the funeral.'

'Here, I'll read you the letter.' I reopened the neatly-written envelope.

Dear Mrs King,

My name is Alexandra Arrington. I daresay you don't recall me. I was a few years below you at school and remember when your father took you out at fourteen to be educated at home. I knew that you were a good scholar and imagine you were disappointed to leave. If so, I understand very well as my father also feels girls' education is unimportant.

'My school was for ladies,' I explained. 'But not for rich ladies. And the Arringtons are *very* rich. Partly because her father doesn't waste money on trifles like governesses.'

I am writing to you in confidence as I don't know where else to turn. I recognised you at the masquerade ball. Not immediately of course, but I saw your hair and then heard your voice and knew it was you. In school I looked up to you a great deal as you were always so confident and determined. I found out that you are now Mrs James King and intended to renew our acquaintance before the dancing commenced, but it was a lively evening and the moment did not arise.

However, I have learnt that you have experience in puzzles and since Toby's death I have not known whom else I could ask for help. No-one knew how I felt about Toby, not even he. We talked a great deal but he saw me as nothing more than a sister. I knew, or thought I knew, his innermost worries, but I never realised he had the slightest interest in firearms. If he had, then I cannot see him as anything other than scrupulously careful. I cannot think how his death came about. It would put my mind at rest to know that it was an accident, however unlikely. The alternative is unthinkable.

I looked up from the letter. 'How strange,' said Connie.

'Yes, isn't it.'

The sun was getting warmer and Bee was becoming fractious, squirming and twisting as Nanny put her in the perambulator.

'She's tired,' said Connie. 'I shall be told off for having her out in the sunshine.' She sighed. 'Tell me, Katherine, how are you feeling? Are you ready to start investigating again, just the two of us? Or is it all too much after what Mr Maynard put you through?'

I shook my head. 'I haven't had the chance to tell you, but James made me go back through that awful interview word by word.'

Connie was aghast. 'How terrible of him!'

'No, it was the right thing to do,' I said. 'I was so angry and humiliated, I had done the one thing a good detective should *never* do.'

'Which is?'

'Fail to listen properly.'

Connie frowned. Nanny was pushing the perambulator towards us. A thin wail leaked from within.

'I realised, when I went through the meeting with Mr Maynard, that what he was saying was not the same as what he said.'

Connie's expression became even more puzzled. 'He didn't really dismiss you?'

'Oh he dismissed me all right and his hands were absolutely tied. I realise now he was furious to have to do it. And suspicious about something — but not me. His last words were *Take care and keep your eyes open.* I thought he was just being polite and hoping I'd find another position, but he wasn't, was he? And the more I think about it, the more I wonder what I was supposed to have witnessed that was so debauched. Half of the best society was there — the younger ones, certainly — and nothing happened but dancing and dressing-up. That happens in country houses, town mansions and church halls every week. Then I remembered what Mr Templeton said about being asked to put on a tableau vivant. Do you think there's any connection?'

'To your dismissal, or to Toby Langland's death?' Connie looked sceptical. Nanny arrived with the perambulator and Connie cooed at her daughter. Bee's grumbles decreased a little, but not a great deal.

'Both, perhaps,' I said. 'After all, if a guest can be threatened with ruin for attending the ball, then how much worse might it be for one of those who helped to organise it. Perhaps it's time for another visit to the Merrymakers.'

'I don't know,' said Connie, looking anxious. 'I couldn't possibly take Bee to a music hall.'

'Garn with you, Miss C,' I said, putting on my best Cockney accent, 'they'll eat her up. But we'd better get moving if we want to see them before the matinée starts.'

CHAPTER 7
Connie

As it turned out, Katherine and I called at the Merrymakers alone. Bee was becoming fractious, and so Nanny had offered to walk her home. 'It's the best thing, ma'am. That way she'll have the chance of a nice nap in the fresh air.'

'I suppose so,' I said, with rather bad grace. 'I mean, thank you, Nanny.'

I was torn between accompanying Nanny or going to the Merrymakers; but Katherine had prevailed. 'Come along, Connie, it'll be like old times,' she had said, with an air of authority and a distinct gleam in her eye, and I had had little choice but to agree. Once we were in the cab, she fixed me with a most businesslike expression. 'By the way, there's something else I forgot to tell you.'

'Really?'

'Yes,' said Katherine. 'Mr Maynard arranged for my personal file to be sent to me. All sealed with wax and everything.'

'So you haven't been dismissed, not really,' I said. 'If Mr Maynard's spirited your file away, then he probably doesn't want anyone to know the sort of work you've been doing. Which probably means that he wants you to come back and do more of it in the future.'

'Do you think so?' Her voice was doubtful, but her eyes shone.

'You should give him a run for his money,' I said with a grin. 'Do be sure to tell him that you've had to return to the music hall. Times are hard, don't you know.' And I tipped her an outrageous wink.

***

The matinée was in full swing by the time we arrived at the Merrymakers, but Ron waved us through the doors anyway. 'What time d'yer call this?' he grumbled, but he was smiling. 'Good to see yer again. Box five's free if you want ter watch a bit, but if I know you lot, you ain't here for relaxation.'

We trooped to our box, and found Dan Datchett finishing his comedy act. I was tempted to put my fingers in my ears before reminding myself that I was a grown woman.

Mr Templeton strode on stage, shaking hands with the departing comedian. 'And now,' he said conspiratorially, gazing round the audience, 'be prepared for the astonishing revelations of Madame Cravatini!'

The lights dimmed, and the stagehands carried on a small, covered table and chairs as a veiled woman walked on stage. The lights rose a little as she took her seat facing the audience, and two respectable-looking women claimed the chairs on either side of her. 'Let us begin,' she said, in dramatic tones, and put back her veil to reveal a pale face and huge, dark-rimmed eyes.

My eyes narrowed. 'That's Selina, isn't it?'

'I believe so,' said Katherine, smiling.

Madame Cravatini proceeded to astound her clients by offering them advice from the spirit world of a surprisingly down-to-earth nature — 'wear wool next to your skin' and 'avoid draughts' were two of the pronouncements uttered in reverent tones and with a faraway gaze. Meanwhile, stagehands with fishing rods wafted scarves across the faces of the shocked clients, while another, clearly visible under the table, alternated between tipping the table alarmingly and tickling the clients' ankles. The act ended with the production of a large stuffed cat, introduced as Madame Cravatini's deceased pet Tiddles, which was placed on the table and spoke rat and fish-related wisdom to the rapt attention of the clients. Selina and her stagehands (and Mr Templeton) brought down the house. The audience stamped their feet and roared for more.

'I don't think I could stand another moment without my ribs cracking,' Katherine said, through tears of laughter.

Selina curtseyed to the audience and promised them more revelations after the interval. 'Come on,' I said, rising, 'we've got a job to do.'

***

The corridor to the backstage area hummed as we hurried down it. Performers rushed into the dressing rooms, pulling bits of costume off, all talking and laughing. I almost missed it; until I remembered how I had never been part of the banter, but the quiet woman in the corner, watching Katherine shine.

'Look 'oo it is!' Selina shrieked. 'Caster an' Fleet are back! Come to congratulate me, 'ave you?'

'I can't think where you got the idea from,' grinned Katherine.

'Me neither, Miss Caster, me neither.' Selina bustled us into the dressing room and waved her hand at a huddle of chairs in the corner. 'Now you'll 'ave to talk while I titivate meself, cos I'll be dancing before Madame C comes back on.' She grabbed a short, sparkling costume from the rail and hitched up Madame Cravatini's flowing robes.

Katherine took a deep breath. 'Do you know of any, erm, invitations to perform at a ball? A masked ball?'

'Can't say I do,' came the muffled reply as Selina hitched the robe over her head, emerging like a sequinned butterfly. 'Ellen?''

'Yes?' Ellen Howe stepped carefully around Selina's discarded robe. 'Hullo again.' She smiled a shy greeting and shook our hands with her own little one.

''Ave you been approached to do a turn at a masked ball?'

Ellen shook her head. 'I remember Mr T growling about something like that, though,' she said in her slow West Country drawl. ''E saw someone out of his office proper sharp, he did, and when the cove'd gone, he said "Them posh folk think they can borrow my people with a snap of their fingers. Must think I came down in the last

60

shower, the carryings-on they get up to with their posing. Masked ball my a —"' She grinned. 'Well, you can imagine.'

'I can,' said Katherine.

***

'A tabloo viv-*ant*,' said Mr Templeton, stabbing the last syllable with his cigar. 'Why yer askin'?'

'An unexpected death,' I said.

Mr Templeton whistled, and stuck the cigar back in his mouth. 'Of an actress?'

'No, no,' said Katherine. 'There wasn't any tableau. Well, not that we saw.'

He guffawed. 'I don't suppose you did. Behind closed doors was what the johnnie said to me. Very exclusive and private. Them's far worse.'

'In what way?' I asked.

Mr Templeton regarded me with some pity. 'And you a married woman now.' He leaned forward. 'In a tabloo vivant, the girls are naked as the day they was born. And that ain't the 'alf of it.'

I recoiled as if he had pushed me. 'Good heavens!'

'Which is why I sent him off with a flea in 'is ear,' said Mr Templeton, leaning back in his chair. 'I've got enough to worry about without sending my girls to be ogled at best and probably much worse.'

'What did he look like, this man?' I asked. 'Was he fair-haired, tallish, well-spoken, around my age?' *Please say no*, my thoughts screamed. The thought of Toby Langlands being mixed up in it. I remembered his stiff retort about being front of house only, and hoped it was true.

61

'Nah,' said Mr Templeton. ''E was a runty dark sort of chap, forty if he were a day.' I tried not to show my relief. 'Now if that's what you came for I 'ope I've given satisfaction, but I've got a music hall to run.'

I checked my watch and gasped. 'Just look at the time!' I imagined Bee looking for me at her dinner, at bath-time, at bedtime —

'You're not staying for the second half, I take it,' said Mr Templeton, drily.

'Please excuse Miss Fleet,' said Katherine; we still stuck to our aliases in the music hall. 'Before we go, could you tell us the name of the man who came to see you?'

Mr Templeton's eyes crinkled at the corners. 'I certainly can, but it won't 'elp you.'

'Why not?' asked Katherine, rather indignantly.

''E said 'e was called John Smith. Now if that ain't a sign of being up to no good, I don't know what is.'

***

'I didn't find anything out from the girls,' I said, as the cab sped across Lambeth Bridge. 'Did the stagehands say much?'

'Everything's much the same,' said Katherine. 'Still moaning about pay, looking for extra shows to take on —'

'About the masked ball, I meant.'

'Yes, of course,' said Katherine. 'A couple of the young stagehands said someone came up as they were leaving one night and offered them a pound each to do some private work at an event. "You two are the best I've seen," he said, apparently. When they asked what the work was, he wouldn't say anything except that their boss didn't need to

62

know, so they told him to — what did they say? — "sling his hook".' She laughed. 'I think Dan and Jerry were a bit cross he didn't ask them.'

I tried to imagine Jerry juggling at the masked ball, but my brain wasn't up to it. 'It looks as if we've hit a wall,' I said.

'On this particular line of enquiry, perhaps,' said Katherine. 'But there's plenty more we can work on. How Lord Marchmont found out I was at the ball, for one. I'd like to work that out very much.' Her hands balled into fists.

'Whether there was a private room at the ball,' I said. 'And if so, what happened in there.' An image of a cross swan popped into my head. 'I wonder…'

'What do you wonder?' asked Katherine.

'Who, more like. I could be wrong, but . . . Archie Bellairs? He went missing and then said he went home early.'

'Oh!' Katherine's hand went to her mouth. 'But would he tell us if he did go in?'

'I doubt it. So we need to find another way to get the information.'

'We do.' Katherine smiled. 'And as you know Maisie Frobisher I think that's a job for you, Connie.'

'I'll see what I can do.' Katherine seemed to have returned to her position of command very readily.

'Excellent. I shall call on Alexandra Arrington, and hear what she has to tell me about Toby.' Her smile broadened to a grin. 'Caster and Fleet are back on the case!'

CHAPTER 8
Katherine

'Well, this is very nice,' said Father, taking a macaroon and popping it in his mouth.

James nudged my foot with his and put his teacup on the low table. Glancing at him sideways, it was hard to tell if my husband wanted to laugh or had a pain. I never trusted him when his face looked so serious. Any minute now he might say something embarrassing and part of me wished he'd just do it, if only because the atmosphere in the room was more poisonous than marsh gas.

He turned to Nathan. 'I gather you are coming along great guns, young man, supporting your uncle,' he said. 'Have you a new adventure?'

'Prehistory,' muttered Nathan. His ears went pink.

'More stuff and nonsense,' said Aunt Leah. 'My dear late husband would be appalled. Dino-allsorts, he called them. People dig up cattle bones and horses' heads, put them together in unlikely combinations and pretend they were once real.'

'My word,' said James. 'Have you seen the dinosaurs at Crystal Palace? I didn't know cows grew so big in Kent. No wonder you moved to London.'

Aunt Leah clenched her jaw so hard I feared it would break. 'Behemoth existed once, and of course so did Leviathan, but neither swam around our sceptred isle.'

'I didn't know Behemoths could swim,' said James. 'Did you see any swimming in Weymouth, Katherine?'

'Katherine should not have been idling in Dorset. She should have been here, allowing me to explain to her how to set up a home for her husband,' Aunt Leah said. 'I'm hoping that she has finally lost any sort of inclination to work either for her father or in a typing pool —' she might as well have called it a den of iniquity — 'and takes on her proper mantle as wife and hopefully mother. She is a young lady and should not work.' Aunt Leah smiled a tight, smug little smile. 'Her humility would have been better demonstrated by accepting her lot and cutting her cloth accordingly.'

I caught sight of Nathan's expression and bit back my planned retort, that perhaps I should have followed her example and found a richer relation to move in with. I prodded my husband under cover of putting my cup down.

'I think we had better take our leave,' said James, rising. 'We both have busy days tomorrow.'

'And really,' said Aunt Leah, 'I don't understand why you gentlemen of private means feel the need to work. Roderick is only pursuing a ridiculous hobby, but you, James, wallow in squalor.'

'I prefer to think of it as exposing the plight of the poor,' remarked James.

'I have no desire to read about the idle poor. The rich have a right to their comforts and the worse-off should trust their betters to know what's right.' Aunt Leah put her nose in the air. 'Another thing, James. There is a house for sale around the corner, which would be much more cosy than a place in Town. Won't you consider it? I could keep Katherine company during the day and train her properly. Alice has allowed far too much laxness, particularly in respect of managing the staff.'

'More hot water, madam?' said Ada, appearing silently and making her jump. James and I rose to leave before she poured it down my aunt's neck.

A few moments later, settled in a cab, he watched me kick the seat opposite until I saw the funny side of things. 'Your father is annoying, but has a certain charm. Your aunt is . . . unprintable.'

'I keep hoping for another relation to come out of the woodwork and take her away,' I said. 'Although that would mean Nathan would go too, and then Father would be seeking an assistant again. I don't think I could face another magic-lantern tour. Are you really particularly busy tomorrow?'

'I shall be wallowing in squalor. Maria told me of another sweatshop. I shall investigate and conduct surreptitious interviews, with a view to exposure. The person it appears to belong to also owns a few of the least savoury slums.'

'Appears to?'

'Yes, I have a feeling he's nothing but an agent. A worm, but an agent worm working for some rich snake who either doesn't know how he gets his money or doesn't care.' He paused. 'I do check my family's investments are above board, Katherine, and I know Albert does too.'

'I never doubted it.' I sighed. 'In contrast, while you're mixing with the desperate, I'll be having coffee with Alexandra Arrington in Mayfair. It's strange that she should have been so open in a letter. I can't remember her well at all. I suspect my morning will be a lot duller than yours.'

'Maybe, but you'll have better coffee,' said James. His fingers idly wound a loose curl at the nape of my neck. 'Mrs King,' he said. 'Do you remember when you complained about my kissing you in cabs without making my intentions clear?'

I giggled. 'Oh dear, Mr King, I barely recall. It is so long since you attempted it.'

'I feared that might be the case,' said James, his voice muffled as he drew closer. 'I think I should remind you. It's rather a long journey home, and I'd hate you to be bored.'

***

Alexandra, head down, twisted her hands in her lap. She had said nothing except greetings since the maid had withdrawn. Despite the thin drizzle outside which obscured the light, the morning room was delightful, with a wallpaper of hummingbirds, and dainty-legged Georgian furniture polished to gleam like agate. A Berlin-work fire screen, intricate in pastel wool, sat in the hearth beside me.

I sipped my coffee and looked more closely at it.

'Is this your work?' I asked to break the silence.

Alexandra raised her head. 'Yes.'

'It's exquisite.'

She shrugged. 'I've little else to do.'

I had cast my mind back and recalled a small dumpling of a girl two years younger than I, with mouse-brown hair. In adulthood, however, Alexandra was fairly tall and slender to the point of boniness. It could not have been down to loss of appetite from grief. She was far too thin for that. I wondered if she was one of the 'starving girls' I'd heard about. Her eyes, which sparkled with tears, were set in dark hollows.

'Miss Arrington…'

'Oh, do call me Alexandra. May I call you Katherine?' I nodded. 'That is a very pretty outfit you're wearing. I do so love that soft dove grey and the trim.'

'Thank you,' I said. It was one of Maria's triumphs. The leg-of-mutton sleeves were proportioned perfectly for my stature, and the square lapels were trimmed in white ribbon. The front of my gored skirt divided to reveal a white underskirt. 'My dressmaker is Mrs Edwards of Pimlico. I have one of her cards if —'

'Thank you. Would she do home visits?'

'Yes. Alexandra, I'd like to say how sorry I am about the death of Mr Langlands.'

Alexandra twisted in her chair and dabbed her eyes with a handkerchief. 'You must wonder why I contacted you and was so frank.' I followed her gaze to the garden. In the middle was an odd stone structure a little like a

Japanese temple. 'It's a shame the rain hasn't lifted. I would have liked to show you our tiny folly. The only one in this part of London. Father had it built to amuse Mother. She did so like *The Mikado*. It was the last entertainment she left the house to see, and she can see the folly from her bedroom now she's an invalid.'

'The rain's not so bad,' I said. 'Shall we risk a little dampness?'

The folly was cold and damp. I didn't dare to sit or lean for fear of dirtying my dress but Alexandra didn't seem to care. She sat on a low bench.

'My mother and Toby's were girlhood friends,' she said. 'He and I played together as children and kept acquaintance through our families. He was wonderful. Did you know him?'

'Not really, I'm afraid.'

'He was so clever, and funny, and wise.' Her voice faltered. 'He was so pleased the ball went well. He told me everything.' She wiped her eyes again. 'Or I thought he did. He and his mother often visited us and sometimes, when our mothers were talking, we would sit here and he would tell me his plans and dreams. He longed for someone to share his life with. I —' She came to a stop. There was an utter stillness about her as she forced her face to be expressionless.

'He'd have realised you were the person for him one day.' I said. I had no idea if it were true. It didn't matter now and it might give her comfort. I imagined her following him around, absorbing every word, longing for the scales to fall from his eyes so that he could see her for

69

the loyal wife she could be. But a young man's longing for a wife seemed unlikely as a reason for suicide. No one had suggested he lacked friends in general, and he wouldn't have been chosen to arrange invitations if he wasn't sociable.

'Our mothers would have liked a match,' Alexandra continued. 'But mine is, as I say, confined to bed and Father wants me to stay home and be her companion until I find a match he prefers.' She glanced up at me. 'Please don't misunderstand me, Katherine. I love my mother, but I always hoped that one day I'd have a home of my own with my own rules — or rather the rules of a different sort of man than Father. It took all Toby's persuasion to get me to go to the ball. I didn't even have time to arrange an outfit. I simply wore a white dress and mask and a brooch with an owl on it, and told people I was Athene.'

'See,' I said. 'He must have cared for you.'

'I never doubted he cared.' She sighed. 'But it was never in quite the right way.'

I pondered. Outside the folly the sun had come out but the shrubbery dripped. As with all London houses, the garden was tiny. There was barely room for the roses and bushes, let alone an incongruous stone structure.

'Why did you ask me to help?' It seemed harsh but I needed to know.

'It was something that came up once when I was admiring some tulips. Toby mentioned a discussion he once had with your friend Mrs Lamont.' That sigh again, and a slight narrowing of the lips. Now I remembered the way Toby had looked at Connie at the ball, and a hovering figure with an unusual brooch nearby. I hadn't thought much of it at the time, too busy smiling to myself as Albert stepped in to claim his wife, as if Connie would ever look at anyone else. 'In female circles there were rumours that you two were more intrinsically involved in solving one or two crimes than the papers would have us believe. Men in general, of course, wouldn't countenance it, but Toby…' Alexandra's gaze moved from the floor to the garden. A cat jumped down from a tree and strolled over to be petted.

'Yes?' I encouraged.

Alexandra stroked the cat's head, then looked up. 'I saw Toby two days before his death. Until then he had been so thrilled with the success of the ball. He had received praise for his efforts and positively glowed. Another is planned, did you know?'

'Yes. Who asked him to organise the invitations?'

Alexandra lifted her hand from the cat as if it had scratched her. It hadn't. 'Oh, I'm not sure. Someone important. But anyway, the last time I saw him, Toby seemed less confident and when I mentioned the ball, he changed the subject. I wondered if a mistake had come to light; perhaps something to do with the invitations.'

'Was Lord Marchmont's name mentioned?'

'Isn't that the minister with the old-fashioned views? Toby would never have included him! But if he'd been invited by someone else, oh dear!' A rueful laugh escaped her lips.

'Why? What happened that would have particularly shocked him?'

'Oh everything. Dancing. Music. People having fun. I

71

met his daughter once. Her life made mine seem positively frivolous.'

'But Toby was upset?'

'Yes. He asked if I thought you were more damned by following your conscience or by keeping quiet. I told him I couldn't imagine him ever doing anything less than noble. He asked if I'd noticed you and Mrs Lamont and I said yes and that I had once known you a little. He said that if anything bad happened, I should call on you. It seemed so odd. If I were troubled I would talk to him — except about how I felt, of course. And then he died.'

'What had prompted his question? Did he tell you that?'

Alexandra frowned, clenching her hands. 'I keep trying to recall. He said —'

'Alexandra!' A booming voice made us jump. A tall, spare, immaculately-dressed man strode across the lawn. 'Why are you hiding here? Your mother needs you.' He saw me, and his next words were delivered in a lower tone. 'Ah, good morning, ah…'

'This is my friend Mrs King, Father.'

He raised his eyebrows a tiny amount, then half-bowed to me. 'I'm sorry, Mrs King, but my daughter is required within. I am afraid your visit must be curtailed. Have you a carriage waiting?'

'Mrs King came by cab, Father,' said Alexandra. 'But perhaps our carriage could take her back to —'

'I shall be using it, Alexandra. However, we can arrange another cab. Come along, now.'

Alexandra's face became still, as if she didn't dare to

risk any sign of irritation or distress. 'I shall ask Phoebe to hail a cab for you, Katherine.' Her voice was perfectly modulated.

I shook her hand. 'Don't worry,' I said. 'I'd like to walk. It's a fine day.'

Alexandra's father bowed to me once more. 'I must bid you good day, Mrs King, I'm afraid I have business to attend to. I do hope you will return, but I'm sure you understand that Alexandra's mother must come first.' He turned and stalked down the hallway.

A moment or two later the front door shut behind me and I stood on the pavement feeling annoyed and small in a number of senses. A cab approached, but I waved it away. It was two miles to Simpson's where I'd arranged to meet Connie for luncheon. The walk would do me good.

Now I walked towards the Strand, lost in my thoughts. It was very busy. Ladies walked with their maids or male escorts. Men bustled or ambled depending on status. People jostled me. Parasols, elbows, briefcases and handbags bumped and jabbed. It seemed warm and yet I felt clammy and nauseous all of a sudden. Then a new thought broke into my musings and despite the queasiness I wanted to dance. Perhaps at last…

I walked into Simpson's smiling at my fancies and expecting the concierge to smile back, but instead he blanched and his mouth dropped open.

'Madam! Mrs King!' he said. 'What has happened? Sit down.' He ushered me to a chair and hissed at a pageboy. 'Henry, find a doctor and call the police.'

'I don't understand,' I said, but I was glad to be seated.

'My friend, Mrs Lamont —' The clamminess was increasing and the world was blurring at the edges.

'Yes, she's here,' said the concierge, 'but sit quietly. Don't move.'

I swayed on my chair and from a hundred miles away, the concierge spoke again. 'I hope you don't mind, but I'll have to touch you. Oh, and your lovely dress…'

I looked down at myself as his hands pressed against my ribcage. On one side, the dove grey of my bodice was red. The world went black and I heard screaming. I had a feeling it might be my own.

Chapter 9
Connie

'Bed rest,' said Dr Farquhar, severely. 'For at least two days, Mrs King. And no exercise for two weeks. You've been very lucky, but I'm not taking any chances.'

Katherine, propped up in the blue-room bed, turned her head to glare at him, and winced. 'Exactly,' said the doctor. 'If it hadn't been for your corset, things would have been much worse —'

She smiled, carefully. 'I must remember to tell James that.'

'Are you sure you don't want me to wire the paper, and get someone to fetch him?' I asked.

Katherine shook her head. 'He's deep in a slum somewhere, and as Dr Farquhar says, it isn't a serious wound.'

'Yes, but there's your arm, too.' I touched her shoulder, which was done up in a sling. 'And you might be in shock.'

I certainly felt as if I was. I had been sitting in

Simpson's, waiting, when a sudden commotion made me look up. The concierge was leading a small red-haired figure in dove grey to a chair, and with every step the red stain at her waist grew a little bigger.

'Katherine!' I rushed to her, but she did not see me; her eyes were closed, and she looked as if she were about to faint. I moved to support her, but the concierge warned me to stay back.

A doctor had been found taking lunch and was doing what he could. 'Moving her might make things worse,' he said. 'Fetch some brandy, man.' He turned to me. 'Who's her own medical man? And have the police been called?'

He gently lifted her sleeve and revealed a gash on the inside of her arm, which was bleeding profusely. 'Get me bandages, quick!' he ordered. 'Raise her arm over her head, madam,' he directed me.

'Wire Dr Farquhar at Harley Street, please,' I said to the concierge, and took Katherine's hand, which was sticky with blood.

A waiter appeared with a table napkin and the doctor tied it tightly round Katherine's arm, above the wound. I watched, my heart in my mouth, as the thin red stream slowed, glistening in the bright light from the lamps. Already Katherine's face was regaining its normal colour, and she opened her eyes. I held the glass of brandy to her lips, and she managed a sip or two before coughing. 'Ow!'

'Try and stay still,' I said, putting an arm round her. 'What happened?'

She frowned. 'I don't know. I was walking down the Strand, and it was busy with people, but I never felt a thing. I mean, people were jostling, but —' She shivered. 'I don't understand. And I don't want the police — well, not any police. They complicate things.'

Fortunately Dr Farquhar arrived before the police. He assessed Katherine's wounds and spirited us away, instructing the driver to go steady and avoid bumps. Katherine bit her lip as the cab lurched through the streets; but she did not cry out once. 'I'll take her to your house in the first instance, Mrs Lamont, if you don't mind.'

He examined Katherine's arm with pursed lips. 'I'll do as neat a job as I can, but this will need a few stitches.' She gripped my hand hard as the doctor worked on her other arm, and I kept my eyes firmly on her face. I couldn't watch.

Dr Farquhar dressed the wound, and hesitated. His face wore an expression I had never seen on it; embarrassment. 'Mrs Lamont, will you help Mrs King remove her corset. I'm hoping any damage is superficial, but we had better check.'

Katherine held her arm out of the way while I unfastened her bloodstained dress, my heart thumping; but the corset underneath was much less red. 'A good sign,' said the doctor, visibly relieved. 'The blood is mostly from your arm, then.' Katherine's corset had a slight rip at the back, and beneath it a small cut on her waist, which Dr Farquhar bathed and dressed. 'Your whalebone bore the brunt of it,' he said, smiling.

'I'll sort out fresh linen,' I said, rising to ring the bell.

'What sort of weapon was it, doctor?' asked Katherine.

Dr Farquhar considered. 'I suspect a stiletto,' he said,

77

eventually. 'The cuts are very fine, suggesting a thin blade, and I think the intention was to stab. Luckily your corset thwarted them and the blade glanced off to your arm, but the blood transferred to your dress convinced them that the deed was done.' His face had grown serious again. 'Be careful, Mrs King, I beg of you. This was no accident.'

***

Nancy brought us tea, and I made Katherine drink a cup with several spoonfuls of sugar stirred in. 'This isn't quite what I had in mind for lunch,' she said, setting the cup down with a grimace. 'I'd rather they carved the joints, not me.'

'Oh, don't,' I said. 'I still can't believe that someone tried to kill you on a crowded street in broad daylight. And in the Strand, of all places.' I paused. 'How was your morning?'

'Interesting,' said Katherine. 'Apparently Toby had suggested she talk to us.'

'To us?' I echoed. 'But why?'

'Our reputation precedes us,' said Katherine, drily. 'But she thought he might have made a mistake, and the ball went less well than he thought.'

'What sort of mistake?'

'I've no idea. She was quite vague. And also broken-hearted over Toby, the poor thing.' The corner of her mouth turned up a fraction. 'She was a little jealous of you.'

'What?' I blushed. 'I don't know her, and I doubt she knows me.'

'Toby talked about you to her, and I think she saw you

two dancing at the ball.'

'But — but that was nothing!' I put my hands to my burning cheeks.

'I know that. I'm sorry, but I thought I should mention it, just in case.' Katherine paused. 'Anyway, did you manage to talk to Maisie?'

I shook my head. 'I did call but two other people arrived just after me, so I had no opportunity to bring it up.'

Katherine sighed. 'We seem to be stuck. And I might not be able to go to the next ball. I certainly won't be able to dance properly. *A Midsummer Night's Dream* is my favourite of the comedies, too.'

'I'll sit out with you,' I said. 'Or James can, and Albert and I shall try and find the secret room. If there even is one.' I frowned. 'Who will you go as?'

'I was thinking of Peaseblossom,' said Katherine. 'If I'm allowed. But whoever saw a fairy in long sleeves?'

'Your outfit is probably the least of your problems,' I said. 'James will probably stand guard over you with a drawn sword.'

Katherine looked rather dreamy for a moment. 'Who are you going to go as?' she asked.

'I thought Albert and I might go as Titania and Oberon,' I said.

'Don't they bicker too much to be you two romantics?' she asked, her eyebrows raised.

'It's tactical, as well,' I said. 'For one thing, I'm too tall and broad to be a convincing sprite, and also —'

'Also what?'

'I imagine there will be quite a few Titanias. So if one vanishes for a while…'

Katherine gripped my hand with surprising strength. 'You clever thing.'

***

I remembered our conversation ten days later, as Tredwell drove us to the Beaulieu Hotel. Katherine looked beautiful in her gauzy fairy costume, although James had insisted that she wear a very stout corset indeed underneath, as well as a blonde wig. 'If anyone's going to manhandle you, it will be me,' he said, looking stern rather than playful.

I had suggested James's costume myself, and I have to say that it was a triumph. He wore a clean, loose-fitting working man's suit — he had drawn the line at breeches — as Bottom the weaver; but the *pièce de resistance* was the ass's head which was currently on the seat of the cab next to him. 'If you do get a chance to snoop,' I had said, 'no one will know it's you. And you probably won't be the only ass at the ball.'

'I'm sure of that,' said James.

Albert and I, as planned, were a matching pair as king and queen of the fairies, both in flowing pale high-necked robes and crowns. 'I feel an utter idiot,' said Albert, hitching up his robe and retrieving a pipe from his pocket.

'You both look magnificent,' said Katherine. 'Anyway, we'll be masked.'

'In some cases, doubly so,' said James, pulling a black silk mask from his pocket.

This time the lackey waiting for us was dressed in ruff,

doublet and breeches. 'Good evening, ladies and gentlemen — or should I say fairies and asses? You're just in time.' He scanned our invitations and waved us through into the ballroom, which was transformed into an enchanted forest with leafy pillars and midnight-blue hangings spangled with stars. A string quartet played soft chamber music on the dais, and all round us were Athenians, fairies, Pucks and rude mechanicals.

Katherine drew closer to James. 'It's very dark, isn't it?' she said.

Just then the lights lifted a little, the chamber music ceased, and a trumpet blared. 'Good day to you all!' cried a hearty voice, and William Shakespeare himself ascended the stage. 'Our revels now are . . . begun! Lysanders, take your Hermias, Demetriuses, take your Helenas — or it is the other way around?' The audience laughed politely, although I could see people exchanging glances. 'Later we shall have a short play which you might recognise, and there will of course be supper, but first — dancing!' And the quartet struck up a lively polka.

'We'll sit out,' said James firmly. Katherine looked exceptionally mutinous, but he steered her towards the chairs in a way that brooked no argument, his ass's head in his other hand. I hoped that there would be some gentler dances later that she might be able to join in with.

'Would you like to dance?' asked Albert. 'If I can manage not to trip over myself, that is.'

'Perhaps the next one,' I said. 'Come for a walk with me. I want to find Maisie.'

She had said that she would be dressed as Hippolyta —

and sure enough I found Maisie's little form, adorned with a miniature bow and quiver, and next to her the sandy-haired figure of Archie Bellairs, robed as Theseus. 'Beats the swan outfit, Mrs Lamont,' he said, grinning broadly.

'You look very distinguished, Mr Bellairs,' I said, curtseying to him. My hair was down at the back, and I felt rather warm and self-conscious for several reasons.

He performed a jerky half-bow. 'Just you two tonight, then?'

'Well, no.' I swept a hand round the crowded room, and a passing waiter put a glass of champagne in it. 'Oooh.'

'I meant your friend and her husband. King, the newspaper man,' he said, impatiently.

'Oh, I see.' I sipped my drink. 'Perhaps you can hunt for them later. Do let me know if you would like a clue.' Archie Bellairs looked at me sidelong, but said nothing. 'Let's find you a drink, Albert.'

Albert let me lead him round the edge of the room. 'What are you doing, Connie?' he muttered.

'I'm looking at the costumes,' I replied. As I had thought, there were at least three Titanias and also another ass's head in the room, although that one was attached to a man in evening dress. 'But it's Archie Bellairs I'm interested in.'

Albert's eyes were shadowed by his mask. 'Be careful, Connie.'

'I shall be.' I beckoned a waiter and secured a drink for Albert, then took two more glasses from the tray. 'Let's find the others.'

The polka had become a mazurka, but James and

Katherine still sat out. Katherine seemed rather bored, but James was regarding the scene with lively interest, his ass's head stowed beneath his chair. His moustache twitched with amusement. I handed them each a drink, and sat next to James. 'Archie Bellairs is looking for you.'

'Have you told him I'm an ass?' he said, grinning.

'Not yet,' I said. 'But I'm about to.'

His smile disappeared. 'Are you sure you want to do this?'

'You can't leave Katherine,' I said. 'And Albert's too tall.'

'That isn't an answer. Seriously, Connie.'

'Toby Langlands killed himself,' I said. 'I need to find out why. Archie Bellairs has the key to at least part of the mystery. I'm sure of it. Are you ready?'

'I still don't like it.'

'Never mind that.'

***

Albert and I accosted Maisie and Archie, who were revolving listlessly to a waltz. 'May I cut in?' asked Albert, and Maisie accepted with what I thought was rather an excess of enthusiasm, while Archie claimed my hand and had soon whirled me away from my husband.

'It's a lovely evening, isn't it?' I said, concentrating on not treading on my robe. I had worn low-heeled shoes, and the difference it made while dancing was surprising.

'Yes,' said Archie, in my ear. 'I still haven't managed to pick out your friend.'

'Oh, her costume is excellent,' I said. 'But her husband is much easier to find.' I waved to James, who had the ass's head in his hands. He put it on, then waved back.

'Oh! that's good,' said Archie Bellairs, chuckling, and gripped me a little tighter.

We talked about nothing in particular until the dance ended, and I made sure I delivered him back to Maisie, who looked just a little suspicious. 'Till the next time,' I said, curtseying low, and he blushed before Maisie put herself very decidedly in his arms.

Albert wandered in Katherine's direction, and I made for the ladies' lavatory, which was down a small corridor — but as I reached it rough fur brushed my hand. 'Careful,' murmured James. I gripped the ass's head, and peeped round the lavatory door. One cubicle was occupied; otherwise it was empty, without even an attendant, and I dashed in and secured the cubicle nearest the door for myself.

I still have no idea what Maria thought of my request; but she complied. Off came my lovely high-necked, long-sleeved robe, to reveal a loose suit which was the near-double of James's. I rolled down the sleeves and trouser-legs, and twisted my hair up in a knot, then donned the ass's head, adjusting it so that I could see out of the clear-glass eyes. I rolled up the robe and, with a silent apology to Maria, stuffed it behind the high cistern. Hopefully it would still be there later; but I had already taken out Maria's mark with a pair of embroidery scissors. I listened for voices — there were none, nor any close sounds — opened the cubicle door, and grinned to myself at the ass reflected in the mirror. I slipped into the corridor, prepared to boom 'Wrong door!' if needed; but everyone was watching the fun.

I skirted the edge of the dance floor. Katherine and Albert were still sitting together, but James was gone. Surely he hadn't — but a familiar voice cried 'There you are!' and Archie Bellairs was before me.

'You're an elusive fellow, King,' he grumbled. 'Come for a chat, won't you? I know somewhere that's more fun than all this dancing rubbish.'

'All right,' I said, at a pitch which I hoped roughly approximated James's.

'Haha! That head makes you sound mighty odd.' Archie grinned. 'You're all muffled.'

'Yes, I must be,' I said. 'Are we going outside?'

'Better than outside.' Archie Bellairs sauntered to the back of the room and pulled aside the dark-blue hangings. Behind them was oak panelling. 'You like a drink don't you, old man?'

'I do indeed,' I boomed.

'Then we'll find you one, and a smoke too. And maybe something even better.' He knocked on the panelling, a curious little pattern which I stored away in my head, and a moment later a section swung back.

I braced myself for what I might see next — but inside was a small bare room, with a scared-looking little attendant standing by a plain wooden door. 'Is that it?' I asked.

Archie snorted. 'Of course not! That's just a precaution.' He pushed on the inner door and I was met with spirals of pale smoke and a sweet, heavy smell. Through the smoky veil I could make out a row of red velvet divans. Two were occupied by men holding long pipes and gazing at the ceiling. Another woman in a full mask and a short shift sat on a third divan. She was stockingless, and barefoot. When she saw us she reclined against the divan and beckoned us with a teasing finger.

'Get the man a drink, would you,' said Archie. The woman uncurled herself. 'And one for me too. A proper drink.' She nodded, and walked to a door at the back of the room. 'There's more stuff in there too, King, if you like. Everything you could want.'

The woman stopped dead, her hand on the doorknob. 'Come on now,' said Archie, 'get that ass's head off and smoke a pipe with me. I want us to have a little chat.'

'He shouldn't be here,' said the woman. 'It's a mistake.'

'No it isn't,' said Archie, 'I was specifically —'

She grabbed my arm and pulled me towards the door, and I could not resist. The smoke was making me drowsy, though, and the divans looked very inviting. The dancing must have made me tired... 'Come *on*, James!' And she hauled me into the anteroom. I just caught sight of the little attendant's petrified face as he rushed to open the panelling, and then we were back in the ballroom.

'Keep walking,' she muttered. 'Walk with me. What were you doing in there?' She sounded as if she was about to burst into tears.

'I was invited,' I said. I knew her voice, I was sure. I remembered the woman who had left the last event early; the same mask, the same dress. 'I know you.'

'Of course you know me.' Now there was a hint of amusement, even through the distress. 'Is she here?

Neither of you should be here. You're not the right sort.'

'I beg your pardon?' But she gasped, and stopped dead. I stumbled; but strong arms gripped me just in time. James's face swam in front of me.

'James?' The woman looked from one to the other of us.

'*Geraldine...*?' whispered James, an expression of utter shock on his face. But she was already fleeing through the crowded room, and we could only watch as the pale shape flitted towards the mirrored doors, and disappeared.

CHAPTER 10
Katherine

The whirling masked dancers were no longer mesmerising but sinister, weaving in and out, their faces unreadable. Leering mouths, flirting mouths, moving to the deafening music. I felt too tired even to observe properly. I was leaning against Albert now, drained by the pain of the corset pressing on the lacerations in my side, and the ache in my bandaged arm.

We were both tense, waiting for Connie and James to return. I hadn't been able to see Alexandra's slim figure. I thought I recognised the outlines of some of the people I'd met through the Lamonts or James, or seen in the illustrated society papers, but the more I looked the more I wondered if I was right. Short, medium, tall, fair, dark, red-headed. Stout, thin. Elegant, awkward. So many were alike. I couldn't see how anyone, even if they were famous, could be picked out with absolute certainty simply by hair and stature. So how had Lord Marchmont been able to identify me?

Maisie swept up and stood before Albert, head on one side, pouting, coquettish.

'I don't have a partner.' She made a moue. 'Poor unwanted me.'

Albert forced a laugh. 'Hardly that, Maisie. I'd do the honours but this robe is exhausting to dance in. Put me down for something sedate later on.'

'I'll come and find you for Sir Roger de Coverley, then.' Maisie made as if to move off. 'Don't suppose you've seen Archie?' Her tone was offhand.

Albert tensed. 'Not for a while, sorry. To be honest, Maisie, I pity the man who tells you what to do, but please consider cutting your losses. I don't think he's good enough for you.'

'Depends what I want him for,' said Maisie, but she frowned as she marched off.

I leaned close to my cousin. 'Do you think we should see what's happening?'

Albert shook his head. 'Could make things worse.'

'Come away Peaseblossom!' A stranger dressed in shimmering green silk shirt and breeches loomed down and swept me up before I could stop him. Albert reached out but it was too late. I was dragged stumbling into the middle of the dance. My companion pulled me tight and I was forced to look up or be smothered in his chest. His leafy mask covered his face from crown to upper lip. I could tell nothing about him but his height, the perspiration running from under his mask, the alcohol on his breath and the insistent heat of his body. I tried to pull free, but his grip tightened, digging into my wounded side, pulling on my aching arm.

'Don't go, my pretty,' he murmured. 'Stay for some fun.'

He whirled me harder than the music required, clumsy on his feet, knocking into other dancers.

I twisted and winced at the pain. I could see Albert torn between wanting to rescue me and watching for Connie and then a woman wearing little more than a silk chemise weaved through the dancers, unsteady on her feet, pursued moments later by James trying to shoulder his way through the crowd. In the commotion the band stopped playing. People ceased dancing, crashed into each other and fell; the man holding me was knocked from behind and lost his balance. I took my chance, pushed him away, and ran back through the crowd to Albert.

'That woman wasn't Connie,' he said, his face ashen. 'Where is she?'

'James wouldn't leave her in danger,' I said. 'I think I know. I'll find her, you follow James.'

'I can't leave you both.'

The band started playing again and the dancers, chuckling, resumed their dance.

'Yes you can, Albert. And there are places you can't go. I'll find her and we'll wait for you under that lamp.' I squeezed his hand and ran to the ladies' lavatory. An ass's head was cast into a dark corner outside. For a wonder, just one cubicle was occupied.

'Connie?' I whispered.

'Katherine?' Her voice was a little hoarse and more

than a little tearful.

'Yes. Can you come out? There's no one else in here.'

'Can you lock the main door?'

'There's no key, but...' I moved the chair and wedged it under the handle. 'Come out, it's safe for a few moments.'

The bolt slid back and Connie came out, her head and arms caught up in the robe and the trousers showing beneath. Wincing, I reached to help her pull the robe straight and smooth it out. Her face had a slight sheen as if she was nauseous, and her hair had become dishevelled by her struggle with the robe. The door handle rattled and a female voice slurred 'Who's in there? Why's door locked?'

'You look green,' I whispered to Connie.

'Your arm's bleeding,' she whispered back.

'A stitch has burst. It's nothing, but we can't stay in here.'

'I feel light-headed.'

'Are you going to faint?'

Connie shook her head. The door handle rattled again.

'Well, *she* doesn't know that,' I said. 'Chin up, I'm moving the chair. Straighten your mask and pretend you feel sick.'

'I don't need to pretend.'

I led her to the second chair and carefully moved the one under the handle. Another Titania fell into the room, her expression obscured by a mask and intoxication. 'Where's the lavatory attendant?'

I shrugged. 'I don't think there is one.'

'Someone should complain about that door.' She stared at Connie. 'What's wrong with *her*? I need my maid. Tell someone to send Mary. I expect they're all called Mary but it doesn't matter. I feel strange. I feel very —' She leaned over the basin and retched.

Connie swallowed hard as we left the lavatory, letting the door slam behind us. 'We lost Archie. Geraldine was pulling me out of the room and she saw James.'

'Geraldine?'

'Yes, she was in the room. I don't know what's happened to her but something's not right, not at all. James brought me this far and ran after her.' She stopped dead. 'Where's Albert?'

'I sent him after James. Hold on to me, Connie. Lean on my head if you need to. Just mind my wig.'

She gave a small chuckle.

'That's the spirit. Come on, nothing's beaten Caster and Fleet yet.'

'We look a state. Well, I do.'

'It's got rather strange out there. I'm not sure if anyone will notice.'

It might have been my imagination but the atmosphere had changed. It felt electric, nervous. Much of the laughter seemed forced. And while most of the revellers seemed much as usual, with a few clearly intoxicated, others, clearly uncomfortable, were on the point of leaving.

When James and Albert found us Connie tucked her arm into Albert's and leaned against him. I had rarely seen James so furious. He was about to pull off his mask but Albert restrained him. Disregarding etiquette, James pulled me into his arms and held me close.

'Lost your head, darling?' said Maisie as she

approached. The words were humorous but her face closed.

'If you ask me, the whole world has!' snapped James.

Maisie adjusted her quiver. 'If you see Archie before I do, please tell him he's an utter bore and I won't be at home to his visits.'

Albert and James exchanged the tiniest of glances.

'What is it?' asked Maisie.

The double doors burst open and the Masquerade Mob, wearing motley, burst in to collect money. They were deafening with jesters' bells, tambours and pan-pipes.

'We're leaving,' said Albert over the racket. 'There's a cab waiting. I think you two should stay with us tonight, and we'll wire your maid. Let's get Connie into the fresh air, and then we need to talk.'

***

In the Lamonts' drawing room, Albert and I listened to Connie and James's account of the secret room.

'Opium?' I said.

James nodded. 'I'm afraid so. Fortunately Connie wasn't in there long enough to breathe in much of the smoke, and Archie never had the chance to force her to smoke it.'

'I wouldn't know how to smoke a pipe anyway.' Connie said. She looked less green now, having been whisked off by Violet to be sick almost as soon as we arrived.

'You should be in bed, ma'am,' Violet had said when Connie insisted on returning to join us. But Connie had needed to talk. Now she'd told her story she lay back on the sofa, cuddled up to Albert, wrapped in his dressing-gown with her hair round her shoulders.

'Violet's scandalised that I'm entertaining James less than formally dressed, but I don't care. He's family,' she announced. 'Only don't tell Mother.'

She seemed dreamy and sleepy and I wasn't sure it was simply the cocoa she was drinking. Then she sat up as if startled. 'It's just occurred to me. Why would Archie want you to go into that room, James? He knows you campaign against the debauchery of the idle rich.'

James raised his head from his hands. 'I don't know. Did he think I'd keep quiet?' he said. 'I thought it was all to do with illicit gambling. I imagined he was fool enough to think he could fleece me. But now — I sent a wire to my editor as soon as we arrived here to tell him I had a story about drug dens to discuss. I swear, Albert, I thought it was nothing worse than gaming. If I'd known opium was involved I'd never have agreed to Connie taking my place. And to see Geraldine like that...'

'Like what?' Albert and I said together.

No one had explained about Geraldine yet. For all Connie's vagueness and James's anger I could tell they were upset, not with Geraldine but on her behalf. Something terrible must have happened.

'If she hadn't been there, goodness knows what would have happened to Connie when they removed that ass's head,' said James. 'She thought Connie was me and she wanted to protect us. She might not like us much but she doesn't want us involved.'

'But what was she doing there?' I said. I recalled the figure stumbling through the dancers, virtually naked, her

94

hair flowing. 'And what's happened to her?'

'I wouldn't wish opium addiction on my worst enemy,' said James. 'If you'd seen what it does to people…'

'You think she's an addict?'

'I fear so.' He stood up and paced. 'She must have built up a resistance to be able to keep her senses in that room. I tried to stop her. I was terrified what would happen to a woman dressed like that out alone at night. No matter what had happened in the past, I would have found a way to help her. But I was too late.'

He stopped, and I put my arms around him. 'You did your best. She had a head start, didn't she?'

'It wasn't that,' said James. 'Archie must have come out of a different door. He bundled her into a cab. There was nothing I could do. But tomorrow we'll find her,' he said, kissing the top of my head. 'We'll find her and help her and then we'll find Archie and get him arrested. I don't know what for, but there has to be something. We'll do that, shan't we Katherine?'

'Of course we shall.' I leant against his chest. I caught Connie's eye and could tell she was pondering the same thing. Geraldine Timpson had tried to destroy our happiness, and she had been involved in treachery and scandal. What if nothing had changed?

***

I don't think any of us slept well. We met at breakfast, sober-faced, James and I back in our party clothes and Connie still wan with dark circles under her eyes.

'What shall I tell Maisie?' she said.

'The truth,' said Albert. 'She will manage. She's

strong.'

I put down my knife and fork. I had no appetite. I jumped when Nancy burst into the dining room brandishing a wire. 'It's for you, ma'am,' she said to Connie.

We watched her open it. Her eyes scanned the contents, and she gasped.

'What is it?' said Albert, half-rising.

'It's from Chief Inspector Barnes,' she said. 'He wants to come round and speak to me. No…' Her eyes met mine across the breakfast table. 'To us. Geraldine Timpson's been found dead.'

CHAPTER 11
Connie

We had been sitting in the dining room with the Chief Inspector for twenty minutes. Albert sat next to me, my hand clasped in his. Katherine and James were on the other side of the table, still in their costumes. Katherine's dress, so pretty and floaty in the lamplight last night, was crumpled and gaudy today, and James looked ill-at-ease in his weaver's suit. James, who was always so sure of himself.

The Chief Inspector had come to us because he thought we might remember something about Geraldine from our dealings with her the year before. But when he heard what we had to say about the night before, his manner changed. He cross-examined James, picking over his words, taking one up and turning it this way and that in yet more questions. He listened to James and Albert's assertions that Archie Bellairs had taken Geraldine away in a cab, and carefully dismantled them. Had they seen his face? Was he masked? Was he wearing a costume? How many men were dressed similarly at the ball? 'Whereas you, Mr King,' said the Chief Inspector drily, 'say that you chased Mrs Timpson across the dance-floor, and subsequently pursued her out of the hotel. How do I know you didn't follow her home?'

'Why would I tell you any of this if I had?' asked James, struggling to maintain his composure.

'You knew that I'd find out about the Beaulieu eventually,' replied Chief Inspector Barnes. 'Now perhaps you would like to explain why you chased after her.'

'How did she die?' asked James, his voice harsh in the quiet room.

'She was found by a neighbour this morning. The door to her lodgings, where she lived alone, had been left ajar. When the neighbour entered Mrs Timpson was in her bed. Next to her was an empty glass, and an empty bottle of a sleeping draught.' The Chief Inspector studied us all in turn. 'The doctors are conducting tests, but the circumstantial evidence is pretty clear, I would say.'

'An overdose,' said Katherine.

'I imagine so,' said the Chief Inspector. 'Now, back to my original question, Mr King. Why were you pursuing Mrs Timpson last night?'

James looked at me as if he were asking permission to tell the truth. I closed my eyes, and for that moment the world I knew and was part of, a world of afternoon tea and visiting cards and lunch at Simpson's, was gone. I opened them, and I could not tell if it had returned or not. I met James's steady look, and nodded.

'I was pursuing Mrs Timpson,' he said, 'because I thought she could give me useful information.'

'About last year's case?' said the Chief Inspector. 'That's done and dusted. She had a lucky escape, but there was nothing else to be revealed, surely?'

'It's not that, Chief Inspector,' I said. 'Geraldine Timpson ran when she saw James because she realised that the person she had rescued from an opium den wasn't James. She had made a mistake.'

Chief Inspector Barnes gave me a steely look. 'Who was this mystery man, then?'

'It was me.'

**

'An opium den.' Chief Inspector Barnes regarded me with a face that gave nothing away. 'You're saying that there's an opium den at the Beaulieu Hotel.'

'Yes.' I described what I had seen — the long pipes, the strange smell, the two men on their red divans and Geraldine, huddled in a world of her own.

'Well I suppose it's possible, if she'd fallen that low.' The Chief Inspector stood up so suddenly that I jumped. 'Mr Lamont, I'll trouble you for the use of your carriage.' His eye fell on Katherine. 'You can't go outside wearing that. Find something less conspicuous, please.'

Katherine looked dazed. 'We're all going?'

'You are,' said the Chief Inspector. 'I can't make head nor tail of what happened last night, but an opium den I can investigate. And you're all coming because, frankly, nothing any of you say makes sense.'

**

Mid-morning, the Beaulieu Hotel looked like any other genteel establishment, dedicated to hushed service and morning coffee. The Chief Inspector had a word at the desk, and we watched the concierge's expression change from polite welcome to utter impassivity. 'Yes, there was an event here last night,' he said, beckoning to another member of staff to take his place. 'I will show you the room.'

The journey to the hotel was uncomfortable both in terms of space and atmosphere. Katherine had had to borrow a day dress from Nancy, who was the nearest to her in size, and she sat wedged between James and the Chief Inspector in utterly incongruous sprigged cotton, her fingers worrying at a loose thread on her cuff. Her face was strained, and I wondered what sort of picture I presented. I felt oddly detached, as if I might float away at any moment, but Albert still held my hand.

We fell into step behind the Chief Inspector, and the concierge led the way down the corridor, down the steps, until we were reflected in the mirrored doors. 'Here we are,' he said, taking a key from his pocket.

The wooden floor and the dais were the same. The pillars and hangings and twinkling lights were gone, revealing a large square room. The walls were cream-coloured, apart from one oak-panelled wall at the back.

'It was over there,' I said, indicating the panelling. 'There's a secret door. I'm sure of it.'

'There is a hidden door, certainly,' said the concierge. 'It leads to the service area.' He crossed the room and sure enough, I could see the line of the door. He pushed that section of the panelling, and it first went in, then opened outwards.

The door opened onto a corridor set alongside the wall. A kitchen porter hurried past, pushing a trolley. I blinked. On the other side of the corridor, directly facing the room, was a plain, closed door.

'It was in there!' I cried. 'This is different — there wasn't a corridor last night, there was just a little room — but that door is the same.' I walked into the corridor, narrowly avoiding a waiter with a tray of cups, and wrenched at the handle.

It was locked.

'Allow me,' said the concierge, taking a ring of keys from his belt. His voice jarred me in its unconcern. He unlocked the door and opened it.

The door swung back to reveal a room lined with shelves, on which were tureens, platters, sauce boats, and stacks of plates and cups. 'This is where we store our winter china,' said the concierge. 'I keep it locked until we change the china over in October.'

'But — but — there were divans!' I looked about me wildly. 'None of this was here!' I pointed at a door almost hidden by a shelf full of teapots. 'What's behind there?'

'I think we've seen enough,' said the Chief Inspector. 'I'm sorry to have troubled you.' And taking my arm, he led me back into the stripped ballroom.

'It was there, I swear it!' I cried, trying to shake him off, but the grip tightened.

The concierge walked towards the mirrored doors, and waited.

'Did any of the rest of you see it?' asked the Chief Inspector. One by one, the others shook their heads.

'Ask Archie Bellairs,' I said. 'He was in there. He knows.'

'Never you mind about Archie Bellairs,' said Chief Inspector Barnes.

'I do mind!' My voice rose. 'He tried to — to —'

'Connie, please.' Albert reached for my hand.

'I don't understand,' I wailed.

'Neither do I.' The Chief Inspector's voice was very serious. 'Perhaps you can all go through it again.'

***

The Chief Inspector interviewed us separately in the morning room. The rest of us waited in the drawing room, mostly in silence. There wasn't much to say that we hadn't already said.

Katherine went first, and was in there for half an hour. She looked wrung out when she came back. 'He just asked me the same things over and over again,' she said. 'Why did I go to the ball, how I hurt my arm, did I know what you were planning to do.' She turned to Albert. 'He wants you to go in next.'

Albert rose, and bent to kiss my forehead. 'Back soon,' he said, but his smile wavered. When he returned, it was gone. 'Your turn, James.' James grimaced and got to his feet. He looked worried, but determined.

'What did he ask you?' I muttered.

'He was more interested in you and James,' he said. 'Specifically why I'd allowed you to impersonate James and go off with another man at a dance. Put like that, I'm not quite sure.'

'Did you say anything about Toby?'

He frowned. 'Of course not.'

James did not return for an hour. Katherine stared out of the window, picking at her sleeve. She jumped to her feet when he opened the door and threw her arms round him. 'I wondered if you'd ever come back,' she said, her voice breaking.

'Still alive,' James said into her hair. 'He thinks it's an irrelevant mare's nest, although he'd like me to tell the inquest later today that I saw her run from the hotel appearing distressed and take a cab. He suggests I don't mention anyone being bundled into anything.' He glanced at me, and his expression softened. 'Good luck, Connie.'

Walking down the corridor to the morning room, I felt the same dread as I had when answering one of my mother's summonses. The Chief Inspector was sitting at the table, his notebook closed in front of him, and a pen on top.

'Sit down please, Mrs Lamont,' he said. I obeyed.

'I shan't keep you long,' he said. 'You must have had stronger drinks than you realised last night. Why on earth do you think something illicit is happening at the Beaulieu?'

Sir Peter's words rang in my head: *You can be discreet.* 'I'm sorry, Chief Inspector,' I said. 'I cannot break a confidence. Not yet.'

'I really don't know what to make of this,' said Chief Inspector Barnes. 'I expected you to talk about last year's trial, not put all this tarradiddle before me. How can I be certain a woman you saw in a non-existent room was Mrs Timpson?'

My throat hurt when I swallowed. 'Because you know me and I know — knew her. I saw enough of her last year, remember? And the room was there, exactly as I said.'

'Well if it was, it's not illegal and the Beaulieu won't admit it easily, will they?' His voice was almost savage. 'If Mrs Timpson was . . . er . . . behaving improperly for money, that might be another matter, but the hotel is even more unlikely to admit to that. If she was, then perhaps it's no wonder she went home and did away with herself.'

'I'm sorry.' I blinked, and a tear rushed down my cheek.

'I'm sure you are, but in case you've forgotten, there's a dead body on a slab in Paddington. I don't mean to be brutal, Connie, but that's how it is. Whatever happened last night at the hotel — I can't believe any of it had to do with her.'

He sighed, and his stern expression softened. 'I do know you, Connie, and I know you're a truthful woman, but by your own admission you say the party was a little out of hand, there was drink flowing, high spirits and possibly opium. I'm not a fool. I could smell it on the wallpaper. I don't know what happened, but I expect you're overwrought. New mothers and all that.' The Chief Inspector nodded as if that would explain everything.

I opened my mouth to speak and the Chief Inspector quelled me with a glare. 'Mr King will tell the inquest that he saw Mrs Timpson leave the ball in a hurry, and beyond that, it's irrelevant. Don't look for things that don't exist,

Connie. There's nothing to investigate. A straightforward case of misadventure. So no meddling, please, and no baseless accusations. Don't drag that poor woman's name through the mud again.' He held out a hand. 'Shake.'

I shook. 'I give you my word. No baseless accusations.'

The Chief Inspector looked at me keenly. 'I've known you your whole life, Connie.' He stood up. 'Don't disappoint me.'

Chapter 12
Katherine

'I want to come with you,' said James.

We had come home, bathed and changed. Now we stood on the pavement, cold despite the blazing sun.

'It's not your fault, James. The best thing for you to do is meet with the editor and see what he is prepared to publish.'

James said. 'If you're sure…'

'Yes — go.' I kissed him, and watched him walk away.

***

The little row of Paddington houses was neat and respectable. There was nothing to suggest that the people who lived there were anything but hard-working clerks or shop staff, the sort of people who kept London running and yet the people whom Geraldine had once barely acknowledged. According to James she had grown up in a large Georgian house in Oxford. On marriage she had moved to a smart address in London. I doubted she had ever realised that houses came with fewer than five bedrooms and several servants.

It wasn't hard to tell which house had been Geraldine's. A black ribbon was tied in a bow on the knocker. The door was open and an ample woman in a white blouse was standing arms crossed on the doorstep, listening to two other women.

'What's Mr Endsleigh going to say when he comes home?' asked a woman in a faded green hat.

'Poor fellow,' her companion replied, shaking a hat resplendent with silk roses. 'When's he due? Poor Mr Endsleigh.'

The woman on the doorstep sniffed deeply and had opened her mouth to reply when she saw me approach. Her eyes scanned me from top to toe.

'Good afternoon,' she said. 'Can I help you?'

The two others turned and stared.

I bit my lip and made the point of visibly swallowing. 'Excuse me,' I said. 'I know this sounds nosy but I heard something had happened to my friend, and I came to see if it was true.'

'Your friend?' said the woman on the doorstep.

Green-hat raised her eyebrows. 'Thought you said no-one visited Mrs Endsleigh, Eth? Except Mr Endsleigh, of course. And the char what helps the girl what does. Not that she's a visitor exactly.'

'Well,' said flower-hat, 'she'd come down in the world a bit, hadn't she, Eth? That was what you reckoned.'

The woman on the door, Eth presumably, grunted and looked me up and down. 'She had, hadn't she?'

I nodded. 'I couldn't find her, not with…' I let my voice falter.

'Not with her family showing her the door,' said Eth.

I sniffed and wiped my eyes. It wasn't hard to pretend. If that was what had happened to Geraldine…

The two hatted women gasped 'Fancy!' simultaneously.

'It's taken me ever such a long time to find her,' I said. 'My parents didn't want me to look for her.'

'Mmm. Well, you'd best come in.' She ushered me into the house and closed the door on the two women.

Geraldine had done her best with the parlour, which was pretty but mismatched. A well-polished piano stood against the wall, with a photograph of Geraldine on top. She was perhaps twenty, wearing the fashion of ten years ago, and standing in a family group on a terrace, arm in arm with someone I assumed was her father.

'That was a beautiful day,' I said, assuming by the summer clothes and light in the photograph that it had been. 'Her father seemed so fond of her.'

'Perhaps he was,' said Eth. 'But…' She lowered her voice. 'Do you know what she did?'

I longed to ask what, but remembered just in time that I was supposed to be Geraldine's friend, enquiring after her.

'Is my friend in bed?' I asked. 'She hasn't been taken ill, has she?'

Eth sucked her teeth and waved for me to sit. 'Thing is, Mrs, Miss…'

'Miss Caster.'

'Thing is, Miss Caster, I'm sorry to be the one to break bad news, but your friend is dead.'

I rallied my best acting skills and gasped. 'How?' I forced out a sob and put my face in my hands. I wished I could turn tears on and hoped my dry face would be put down to shock.

'Here,' said Eth. 'Don't take on.' She sat beside me on the hard settee and put an awkward, wiry arm around me. 'How close were you to Mrs Endsleigh?'

I frowned. 'I didn't know her as Mrs Endsleigh,' I said. 'I didn't know she'd married.'

'Huh,' said Eth.

I tried my best to look puzzled. 'What do you mean?'

'Listen, miss, you dress as fancy as she did and you sound as fancy, but there's something about you that tells me you're not easy shocked. Are you?'

I shook my head.

Eth scrutinised me. 'Tell me, fancy miss as you are, what would you do if all of a sudden you had no money?'

Without pausing to think I said, 'I'd get a job.'

Eth gave a grim smile. 'You would, wouldn't you. You wouldn't take up with the first man who offered you a home, in return for services rendered but no wedding.'

'I'd rather scrub doorsteps.' It came out before I could stop myself.

'Good girl. There's no good end to being a kept woman. More often than not, the man loses interest when you get a bit long in the tooth. Then it's downhill all the way, and her with —'

She let out a long sigh. 'I'm sorry to tell you this about your friend. I live next door. I own this house and rented it out to Mr E a year or so ago, and he soon brought Mrs E to live here.' Eth settled herself more comfortably. 'Now, he isn't hardly ever here. The perfect tenant, you might say. Mrs E was in and out the first few months, until —' Eth broke off and seemed to be thinking what to say next. 'But in the last month or two there's been another man here on and off, mostly in the evenings. Now I couldn't say if it was him or who it was, but last night she turns up in a cab, hardly able to walk, with a man holding her up. He took her inside and there was shouting. It's a disgrace, drunkenness and rowing like that. I came round this morning to give her a piece of my mind and…' Eth's face changed from belligerence to pity. 'She was dead. You don't take laudanum, do yer?'

I shook my head.

'Don't you start, you hear. I'm not saying she done it on purpose, more likely by accident, but it's a waste. That's what it is. A waste.'

It was. However much I had loathed Geraldine, she had ended up like this. Under the pretence of wiping my eyes, I thought.

'Could it have been Mr Endsleigh who brought her home?'

'Mr E? Not sure. It was dark, wasn't it? Coulda been, I suppose, but 'e 'ad a big cloak on. All I saw was that he was tallish.'

'What does Mr Endsleigh look like?'

'He's got a moustache but then what gent hasn't? Charming. A gentleman. Why he needs a place here I don't know. But it's none of my business as long as the rent gets paid. And Mrs Endsleigh was a one. She didn't know how to boil an egg, nor yet get the dirt out of linen. Mrs Endsleigh might have been someone's wife, but she wasn't Mr E's, for sure. Anyone could see that. I thought she'd gone a bit strange recently, but put it down to the laudanum… Someone brought her home last night, like I said. But this morning she was all on her own. All on her own.' Eth ran her hands over her eyes as if to wipe the image from them.

Someone rapped at the door and yelled 'Coo-eee!' through the letterbox.

Eth swore, then glanced at me. 'I didn't think it would take her long.' She rose and opened the door.

'Here you are, Eth,' said a small round woman in an elaborate hat. She was carrying a baby in a shawl.

'How do, Mrs Tanner,' said Eth. 'You heard the news, then. I don't know when Mr Endsleigh'll be back, but I'll let you know when he is.'

'That's not good enough,' said Mrs Tanner. 'You know and I know the chances are he'll never come back and I've got a living to make. Mouths don't feed themselves.' She held the baby out as if it were a gift. 'Sorry Eth, but I can't look after her for nothing. She's yours till Mr E comes back, and then she's his. Here's the bundle of things Mrs E left with her. It's all there. You can add the care to the rent. I've got a new baby arriving this afternoon and the mother will be a good payer. Mrs E was away with the fairies and you know it. The laudanum would have got her in the end. If he don't turn up, the workhouse'll take her. Chances are she wasn't never his anyway.'

Before anyone could move, Mrs Tanner put the baby

111

and a small bag on the floor and walked out of the house. The baby stared solemnly.

Eth ran her hands over her face again. 'I knew it. I knew she'd do that, the old cow. The baby's not Mr E's, I know that for certain. If it was, he wouldn't have wanted her farmed out. Arrived five months after he brought Mrs E here, bonny as you like. *He* won't take her. And if her family cared, they'd have taken her in themselves. So on top of everything else I'll have to take the baby to the workhouse. What a day!'

'No,' I said. The baby stared at me with large blue eyes. Brown curls peeked from the edges of her bonnet. She looked as if she wanted to cry but was afraid to make a noise. 'Not the workhouse. I'll take her. If Mr Endsleigh comes back, you can contact me here.' I rummaged in my bag for pencil and paper and wrote *Miss Caster, care of Bayswater Road Post Office, London W.*

I picked the baby up carefully and took her bag in my free hand. 'What's her name?'

Eth frowned. 'It's Lucy. Mrs Endsleigh called her Lucy. But you can't —'

'Yes I can. It's the only thing I can do for Geraldine.' And before I could change my mind, I walked out of the house.

***

After five minutes of indecision in the cab, I took Lucy to Mulberry Avenue. James would still be out of contact, and Connie was hopefully getting something useful from Maisie. Aunt Leah was the last person I wanted to see, but I hoped that Father, with his love for wild adventure and illogical decisions, would somehow understand the situation. I had sent an enigmatic wire to Aunt Alice and hoped that she and Mina would be waiting to support me. And if the worst came to the worst, I'd hide in the kitchen with Ada.

Now here we all were in the old family drawing room and everyone was staring at me.

Lucy was asleep, snuggled into my shoulder. The tears in my own eyes were reflected in Aunt Alice's as I said that an old friend had died, leaving a daughter with no father or other family.

'Oh, the poor mite,' she said, coming to lift the baby out of my aching arms.

'The result of sin!' declared Aunt Leah. Aunt Alice glared at her and held Lucy close.

'The result of a biological reaction,' retorted Mina, pouring me a cup of tea.

Aunt Leah's lip curled in disgust. 'That is as revolting if not more so, and you an unmarried woman, Miss Robson.'

'She's delightful,' said Father, coming over to stroke Lucy's cheek. 'Katherine did the right thing. I would be appalled if she'd let the child go to the workhouse with no-one to love her. Leah, I'm ashamed of you. Our Mama would have done exactly the same.'

'Our Mama was sentimental, as well you know.'

'She was a good practical Christian,' argued Father.

'This child is tainted. The result of sin.'

'Whatever her parents did, it is not Lucy's fault!' snapped Aunt Alice. 'I for one would consider it a sin to abandon her to neglect and misery. I would not want to face my maker and say I'd let Lucy go to the workhouse for the sake of my reputation in the eyes of men.'

'If Katherine insists on bringing this child into the family, I could not bear the shame!' declared Aunt Leah. 'I would have to leave and disown you all.'

We stared at her in silence. Even Father.

'I'm not leaving,' said Nathan. 'I've never been as happy as I am here.'

Aunt Leah glared and strode out of the room.

Lucy stirred in Aunt Alice's arms, her eyes opening and filling with tears. She still made no sound.

'Is there a bottle in the bag?' asked Mina. 'Or any feeding tools? She must be hungry by now.'

I opened the bag. Within were a spare set of clothes, some napkins, two bottles and teats, silver feeding tools, a birth certificate naming Mr Timpson as Lucy's father, a sealed letter addressed to Lucy, and a rattle similar to the one I'd given Bee although rather more elaborate. It was designed to be chewed and shaken, though this one had a thicker ivory handle.

The letter said: *My darling Lucy, If you read this, then I am dead. I hope that you are grown up and safe and happy. I am so sorry I could not be the mother I wanted to be. Josiah Timpson will not recognise you. You do not deserve the shame I have brought you. I am sorry I have nothing to give you but what is in this bag. I love you so much. Mother.*

'Won't James be excited?' said Father.

I opened my mouth and shut it again. Then I looked at Aunt Alice. She was crying as silently as Lucy as they

114

gazed at each other. It was so unlikely she would ever have a child of her own. I still had a chance.

I took a breath. 'Aunt Alice,' I said. 'I don't know how I'd manage a baby just now. I don't suppose you…'

She looked up, her face bright with smiles of joy despite the tears and the deep sob that came from her. I caught Mina's eye. I could tell she understood what I'd have given to keep Lucy for myself.

'I'd better go home,' I said. 'James will be waiting.'

***

In fact, as I had hoped, he wasn't. I had washed and changed by the time he got home.

'How did it go?' I asked, before he could ask about my day.

James ran his hands through his dark hair, which had reverted to its morning state of curliness. 'The editor said he'll run something, but not till there's more evidence. He's supporting me provided I don't bring the paper into disrepute. I said I feared someone was trying to discredit me.'

'Why would they do that?'

'I'm not sure . . . but the editor's worried about my articles on slum landlords. There's a bill being proposed to tighten up regulations, and another to make landowners build suitable new housing for the poor when they demolish the old ones. He said what I've written may stir up trouble.' James's gaze was very steady. 'I think someone wants to shut me up.'

CHAPTER 13
Connie

'Look at them,' I said softly, as we gazed at the sleeping babies. Lucy was tucked up on Nanny's bed, a soft toy dog pressed against her face as she sucked her thumb. Bee, meanwhile, was splayed out in her cot like a starfish, snoring gently, with a tiny smear of pureed carrot on her chin.

'I might go to the kitchen for a cup of tea while it's quiet,' said Nanny. She glanced at Aunt Alice. 'I suggest that you ladies rest too.'

Aunt Alice gazed at Lucy. 'Oh, I don't mind,' she said.

'Are you sure you can cope?' I asked Aunt Alice.

Nanny gave a nod of approval. 'Mrs Frampton is managing beautifully,' she said, softly. A shy smile crept across Aunt Alice's face, and her eyes filled with tears.

I took Katherine to my boudoir and rang for tea. 'Now then,' she said as I sat down. 'Tell me about Maisie Frobisher.'

I sighed. 'There isn't much to tell. She's still hopping mad with Archie Bellairs for abandoning her again at the ball, and she isn't exactly pleased with me.'

Maisie had been extremely forthright about the whole affair. 'Archie ought to be on his knees at the chance to accompany me to a ball,' she said indignantly, crashing down her cup. 'A chap like that, with only an MP for a father — what use is he to anyone?'

'In that case,' I said, wondering what opinion Maisie held of my father or husband, 'why did you let him?'

A smile flickered over her face. 'He begged, and I felt sorry for him.' Then her mouth twisted up. 'And then he spent more time dancing with you and asking about your friends than he did looking after me!'

'I'm sorry, Maisie,' I said, seeing that she was genuinely hurt.

'It isn't your fault,' she said. 'He's an idiot. I wish I didn't have to bother with bringing a man along. And if you ever see me with Archie Bellairs again, just shoot me. He's called twice since then, you know, but I am resolutely not at home.'

'Oh dear,' said Katherine, when I relayed the exchange. 'Poor Maisie.'

'Mmm. It doesn't get us much further on, though, does it?' Nancy came in with the tea. 'How is James?' I asked, once her steps had faded down the corridor.

'Sad. Worried. He's attending her funeral today and dreading it.' Katherine poured out for both of us. 'He's upset over Geraldine, naturally. He gave evidence at the inquest, and even though the inspector asked him not to

117

mention the opium den, he's worried that if the police look further into things he may become a suspect. And on top of that, work isn't going well. His editor is blocking him. He won't run anything about the ball.'

'Couldn't he take the story elsewhere?' I asked.

Katherine made a face. 'He could . . . but he feels it would be disloyal.'

'Oh.' A thought had come to me, and I sipped my tea while I considered it. 'Do you know, I don't think I've seen anything about the ball in the newspapers. Considering all the criticism of the last one, you'd think there would have been.'

'I suppose,' said Katherine. 'Then again, the papers are full of the workers' threats to strike, and scaremongering that the country will grind to a halt. A lot of well-off people going to a ball isn't very important, next to that.'

'But someone died,' I said. Poor Geraldine — running for her life, as I now knew. What had she said to me? I had been disoriented, confused, and the tone of her words was clearer than the words themselves. There had been fear, and panic — but also amusement. *Of course you know me.* How sad those words were, now.

Neither of you should be here. You're not the right sort.

'Katherine,' I said, 'will you promise not to bristle if I tell you something?'

She looked at me warily. 'It depends.'

'Geraldine said you and James shouldn't have been at the ball.'

Katherine raised her eyebrows. 'Well I hardly think —'

'But don't you see? Albert suggested to Toby that James

118

could come and perhaps write up the event, and Toby was glad to invite you both, as friends of ours. We got our tickets through Maisie. None of us were on the original guest list. So who was?'

'Ohhh…' Katherine's face lit up. 'Alexandra said she thought Toby might have made a mistake!' Then she frowned. 'But Alexandra wasn't there on Friday, I'm sure of it. I looked out for her specially.'

'And yet she comes from an old-established, wealthy family. You would think she'd be exactly the sort of person they'd want.'

'And if Geraldine knew who they wanted, she was in on whatever the real point of the events is. If it was just donating to charity, they wouldn't have been half so choosy.' Katherine's face took on an abstracted expression. 'I think I can hear crying.'

I started, guiltily, and listened. *Bee*. 'Oh dear. What a terrible mother I am.'

'Don't be ridiculous,' said Katherine. We stood and made for the door. 'Bee is looked after to within an inch of her life. This is important. And I have a feeling that it's bigger, and worse, than a party gone wrong.'

***

Aunt Alice was very firm about taking Lucy home. 'She needs to get used to her routine. And you must come too, dear,' she said to Katherine.

'Oh, I'll be fine,' said Katherine. 'I can get a cab. Or Tredwell could bring me.'

Aunt Alice's face set. 'After what happened I'm not letting you out of my sight till you're safely at home.'

Katherine sighed. 'Oh, very well.' She took her gloves from her bag. 'Please work it out soon, Connie, or I'll die of boredom from being looked after.' But I could see the love in her face as she squeezed her aunt's hand.

No meddling echoed in my head as I sat alone in my boudoir. But we weren't meddling, surely? If only I had someone to talk the whole thing over with — but Albert was in a meeting with Mr Anstruther and Father, and I did not expect him home until dinner. Katherine was with Aunt Alice. James was at work. I felt thwarted at every turn — but I was certain there was a connection between Geraldine's death and Toby's terrible secret.

And then I remembered what Mina had said: young people, rich people, driven to despair. What if there were more? If I had to meddle, then so be it.

Why didn't you come to us, Toby?

He had left nothing behind him concerning the ball; no lists, no papers. Those were the first things that Albert and I had asked for. Either they had been destroyed, or they were kept somewhere else. *Oh, for a list of the guests.* I scrabbled in my bureau, and began to make a list of people I had seen or known to be at either event.

Connie and Albert Lamont, Katherine and James King — not on original list. Yet we had all received tickets for the second event in our own right.

Alexandra Arrington — not at second event

Maisie Frobisher and Archie Bellairs —

Maisie had definitely been invited, and given extra tickets for the first event. Archie, though, had begged her to be allowed to come.

At the second event, Archie had known his way around. He had taken me, as 'James King', into the secret den, he had been familiar with Geraldine, who knew at least some of what was going on, and he had hinted at more behind the next door.

Archie Bellairs must be the key.

But where was he? Albert had made enquiries at Archie's club, and via several generous tips had ascertained that, though a regular attender, Archie had not visited since the night of the ball. Reg and two friends had even watched his rooms for comings and goings, and reported in the negative.

I remembered the Chief Inspector's guarded look when I had mentioned Archie, his 'never you mind' which had made me so angry, and wondered why the inspector had wired me. It couldn't just have been about the previous year's trial. My face went cold. What if he had been told something else? What if they had spoken to Archie? Archie had known Geraldine, he had bundled her into the cab — for all we knew he had killed her. But he wouldn't admit any of that to the police. Archie was not James. And if he had called on Maisie, he must still be at liberty.

Perhaps the Chief Inspector was watching to see what Archie Bellairs did next. That was reassuring, but it didn't get me any further forward. Perhaps I should just try to remember the guest list, and see if I could find any sort of link. I could call on Alexandra Arrington — but given what had happened to Katherine after visiting her, the idea did not appeal. Though of course that was merely coincidence. Plus I didn't know which was her at-home afternoon. And she probably wouldn't talk to me anyway, since Toby had danced the tango with me.

But there might be an account of the ball in the society pages today. I got up and went in search of the *Times*, which I found in Albert's study still neatly folded and obviously unread. I wet my finger and riffled through the pages, scanning the columns. Nothing.

Would a slightly less grand newspaper have covered the event? I summoned Johnson, and asked him to go and buy a range of papers. 'Yes, ma'am,' he said, sounding rather puzzled. He was back within fifteen minutes, and I settled in Albert's desk chair prepared to get my hands filthy with newsprint. At least it would keep me occupied until the dinner bell. I was in no state to be a fit companion for Bee, certainly.

It did not take me long to find it. Not an account of the ball, but something far worse. It was in the *Monitor*, a right-wing paper whose first few pages were taken up with ranting about working men who expected to be treated with kid gloves.

It was a small item near the bottom of what purported to be the society and court page, though it was mostly low gossip. The header was *Pot and Kettle*.

A certain holier-than-thou campaigner, and critic of the so-called 'idle rich', may have to eat his words. A little fairy tells this paper that he was seen chasing a young woman at a fancy ball — a woman, moreover, who was not his wife. Perhaps he wanted to offer her a little of his private income?

'The poisonous little —!' There was no doubt in my mind that Archie Bellairs was behind this. I clenched my fists and banged them on the desk. Not content with taking James into an opium den to do God knows what, he was now smearing his name! Obviously he must be Mr Endsleigh, and was trying to divert suspicion so that he wouldn't have to support poor little Lucy, whoever's child she was.

But then I remembered the description Katherine had given me of the mysterious 'Mr Endsleigh'. He had a moustache, whereas Archie was clean-shaven. What else had been said? Dark-haired, tallish, charming, a gentleman. *Ha, that could be James,* I thought —

No, I whispered to myself. Then little Lucy, with her dark curls, came into my mind, sleeping so nicely in Nanny's bed.

Albert found me at his desk, surrounded by papers, when he came home. 'What are you doing in here, Connie?' he said, laughing. 'It's only ten minutes till dinner —' Then he saw my face. 'What is it?'

'I don't want to believe it,' I said, and my voice was hoarse from crying. 'I *won't* believe it!'

CHAPTER 14
Katherine

Aunt Alice and Lucy, accompanied by Nanny, left me on the steps of my house and sped off to interview a nursemaid for the Frampton household. Lucy had sat on my lap all the way there like the Queen of Sheba, chewing a wooden elephant, sometimes turning her head to stare at me with serious eyes. And then I had to hand her back.

I waved them goodbye until the carriage was out of sight, then wandered into the park and sat down, wondering what to do next. No-one was supervising me. I didn't care what Dr Farquhar said; I could go where I wanted and do pretty much anything. It seemed pointless to return to Geraldine's house. Aunt Alice, Mr Frampton, the vicar and I had gone there the previous day after church to reassure Eth that Lucy was in respectable hands and leave an address for Mr Endsleigh, should he return. Eth was indifferent and simply handed over a bundle of Geraldine's personal belongings which she felt ought to be

Lucy's, including the photograph. It didn't amount to a great deal; a few bits of jewellery, an unfinished piece of embroidery, and some books. Mr Endsleigh hadn't reappeared despite the inquest being reported, and as he'd been late with the rent more than once Eth was planning to change the locks. Geraldine's fine clothes were already being set against any losses.

Under an overcast sky, the little park in Joyce Square was busy. It was pretty with bright flowers and even the threat of rain couldn't dim them completely. Little boys ran with hoops, babies were pushed in prams, their faces half-obscured by lacy bonnets, little girls sat with dollies on the benches, and two round-stomached and artfully-draped ladies were taking a late-afternoon turn round the park. They nodded as they passed. *Good-day Mrs King; good-day Mrs Smythe, Mrs Cornwell.* I had a sudden urge to be anonymous in office clothes, tutting over someone's English as I typed, or to be helping Father on to a train as we headed out for another tour, too busy to notice a world full of babies and expectant mothers.

The house was quiet. I couldn't hear Susan singing as she usually did, nor the bump and clatter of Monday housework which would be behind because of the laundry. Yet the place didn't feel empty, just silent.

I found James sitting on the floor in his study, his collar and black tie discarded next to him. He sat hunched in his shirt sleeves and didn't look up when I sat beside him. I pulled his head onto my shoulder.

'I've given Susan the rest of the day off and told her to go home to her family for the night,' he said. 'She'll come back at six tomorrow morning. We can manage, can't we?'

'Yes, of course we can,' I said. 'Was the funeral very bad?'

James lifted his head and ran his hands through his hair. 'Yes.'

'Can you tell me?'

He didn't speak for a moment and then spoke so quietly I could barely make him out. 'There was virtually no-one there. Just the vicar, me and Geraldine's father. Not her husband nor her brother, none of their male relations or acquaintance. Just the three of us. The vicar said he'd seen her in the church, but she always slipped out without speaking to anyone. I'm not sure if little Lucy is even christened. If she is, it wasn't at that church.'

'Perhaps the midwife did it.'

'Probably.' His fists clenched. 'There was no-one to say a nice word about her. I couldn't because the only nice thing she ever did was get Connie out of that opium den. The vicar didn't know her. He tried his best, but he could have been discussing the cat. Her father *wouldn't*. He sat stony-faced through the whole thing, just as he did at the inquest when they said she died by misadventure. Since he came to both and needn't have, I imagine he feels something, but you'd never know it to look at him. I think he was glad the shame was finally over. Death before dishonour.' His mouth trembled. 'I have seen babies and young brides laid to rest, but I have never been to a funeral so utterly sad. No-one cared about the woman in that cheap pine box.'

I pulled his head close and kissed him. 'Did you

126

mention Lucy to Geraldine's father?' My heart pounded.

James snorted. 'Aunt Alice has his blessing provided she makes no claim on the family. That's not what he said, but it's a politer version of what it boils down to.' He ran his hands over his face again and then raised his head to look at me properly. His mouth dropped open a little and with his thumb, he caught the tear in the corner of my eye. 'Oh Katherine, I'm so sorry. Why didn't you keep Lucy if that's how you felt? It would have been a surprise, but —'

I swallowed the sob. 'Because Aunt Alice can't ever have a child now and maybe . . . maybe one day I'll keep one.'

'Keep one?' James stared and then light dawned. 'You mean — but you never said…'

'It was too soon. I never knew for sure. It was too early to go to a doctor. But twice, I felt different. Things were out of kilter. I thought I'd caught . . . and then a day or so later it was the usual curse only a little more unpleasant. Not much worse, but a little.'

'Why didn't you tell me?'

'It was over before there was anything to say.'

'But afterwards?'

'I am probably imagining things. I didn't want to upset you.'

'Oh, Katherine.' He pulled me close. His tears were in my hair, my tears soaking into his shirt. 'I love you so much. I can't bear to see you so sad.' He lifted my face and kissed away my tears and I held him close and kissed his mouth, his heart beating faster and faster against mine.

***

The doorbell woke us. I was wrapped in James's arms on the floor of the study and my hair was in a tangle. We looked at each other, then down at ourselves.

'I'll go,' I said. 'I can make myself respectable quicker than you can. I'll get a wrap from the bedroom.' I brushed my curls out of my face. 'And maybe a snood.'

The doorbell rang a second time as I arrived at it.

On the mat stood Mrs Buchan's maid. 'This was delivered through the wrong letterbox, Mrs King,' she said, handing over an envelope with a lilac trim.

'Thank you,' I said. The maid bobbed and beetled off downstairs, her back ramrod-straight. I wondered what, if anything, she would say to her mistress.

A few minutes later I sat in the sitting room, now wearing a loose tea-gown and with my hair in a plait, reading the contents of the envelope. *Miss Alexandra Arrington invites Mrs James King and Mrs Albert Lamont to tea.* How odd. My arm ached at the thought of that dark garden and the walk along that road with the hovering mansions. I didn't altogether feel like any more socialising, but it was just possible that this was the only way Alexandra could speak to us. I put the invitation to one side and took up a book.

James had just joined me when the doorbell rang again. 'My turn,' he said, rising. When James returned my cousin Nathan was with him, his face red above his collar and a variety of expressions moving over it like clouds on a windy day.

'Do sit down, Nathan,' I said. 'I'll make tea.'

'I can't sit down,' said Nathan, 'I'm too angry, and —

pah!' He began to pace.

'Oh,' I said, unsure of the correct etiquette in such a situation. 'I won't be long.'

'I feel a fool,' said Nathan when I returned with the tray. He was still pacing.

'Well, feel a fool sitting down with a cup of tea inside you,' said James.

'I'm sure you needn't feel a fool,' I said, frowning at James.

Nathan continued to pace, his fists clenched. 'I'm twenty-one and I'm sick of being told what to do. Father and his stupid rules, Mother and her fussing. *Don't do this, don't do that, those people aren't our sort, that's not proper.* You don't know how lucky you and Margaret are, Katherine. Mother says you grew up able to do exactly as you chose.'

I boggled at the thought that our lives were in any sense free from restriction, but there was no interrupting my cousin in full flow.

'Your father is the most wonderful man. Imaginative, dauntless, not afraid to try new things. Prepared to take risks and face censure.'

'Mmm,' I answered, pouring the tea.

'I had to leave the house, do you understand?' said Nathan. He flung himself into a chair and slammed his fist on the arm-rest. 'I had to go somewhere. I couldn't stay a moment longer. Mother has been unspeakable to everyone for days and today, when I broached a subject very dear to my heart, she — she —' He thumped the chair so hard that I feared either for the armrest or his fist.

129

'Have some tea,' said James. 'Or something stronger.'

Nathan flushed. 'I've never touched alcohol, although perhaps I should! Yes! Bring me brandy!'

'Then again, perhaps you shouldn't,' said James. 'Not in this frame of mind. And you wouldn't want the stuff Susan uses for cooking, you really wouldn't. She also uses it on newspaper to clean the brass.'

'I'd like you to know I don't believe a word of the rumours, Mr King,' Nathan said, eyeing the paper James had tossed on the low table. 'If it's not in the respectable press, I don't believe it.'

'Don't believe what?' said James. 'And you can call me by my name.'

'When I saw that thing in *The Monitor*, I knew it wasn't true.'

'The *Monitor?* That rag? I wouldn't believe that if it said grass was green. It supports the worst of the people I want to expose!' James exploded. 'Why do you read that sort of paper? Do you agree with its political stance?'

'No! No!' cried Nathan. 'Quite the reverse!' He ran his finger round his collar. 'Can you keep a secret?'

We nodded.

'I've always had to find a bit of space away from Mother. I always have, from the minute I was old enough. I started with things Mother would approve of, temperance meetings, lectures on morals, that sort of thing. But she didn't know I was meeting all sorts of people.'

'How do you mean?' I said.

'Well, they weren't *our* sort, you see. There were a lot of working people. People Mother thought were rough.'

130

'Go on,' said James, leaning forward.

'The things I heard shocked me. I didn't know lives like that existed.'

'Was there no poverty where you grew up?' said James.

Nathan went pink. 'Yes, but Mother didn't allow me to be exposed to it. Back in Sydenford, Mother didn't like me mixing with anyone but the better-off. Only we weren't well-enough off to be anything other than on the periphery. It was deadly. But then I met —'

'Sydenford?' interrupted James, frowning.

'I got interested in workers' rights,' Nathan continued. 'I met someone, you see, who explained things. She showed me how to read the papers in a different way. I realised how they can inform or they can manipulate your views. That was when I began to appreciate your articles, Mr K — James. And she and I want to — Well, I have asked her, and when I started to explain to Mother...' His face grew even redder.

James's colour had returned to normal as he listened, and a small smile appeared. 'So, Nathan, can we go back a little? Tell me about your old home in Sydenford. Who's your Member of Parliament?'

'Oh, that's easy,' said Nathan. 'It's Mr Anthony Bellairs.'

I caught James's eye. There was a spark in it which had been lost for days.

'Do you know his son, Archie Bellairs?' I asked.

'Yes, of course,' said Nathan. 'I saw him the other day, in fact. That was when Sarah and I —'

'When? Where?' asked James, leaning forward.

'On Friday evening, at a temperance meeting near Kensington Workhouse.'

'Archie, at a temperance meeting? On *Friday*?' I exclaimed.

Nathan shrugged. 'He's always making speeches about people respecting their betters. Encourages the working class to trust in their landlords and bosses. Mother would love it, but it makes us sick, I can tell you.' He bit his lip and stared into his teacup.

Now it was James's turn to pace. 'But Archie can't have been there on Friday evening. When did he arrive? What was he wearing?'

Nathan shrugged. 'I'm not sure when he arrived; I, um, wasn't paying attention. The meetings start quite late, though, to allow people to come after work. I was talking to my — my friend.' His blush deepened still further then he looked thoughtful. 'When he did speak, Mr Bellairs came out with a lot of hot air about how the better-educated know what's best. But then "better educated" only applies to the rich, doesn't it?' He paused again, frowning. 'Maybe that's why he turned up in his university gown and hood. For all I know, he was dressed as a pirate underneath.'

CHAPTER 15
Connie

'Just — be careful,' said Albert, hovering in the doorway as I screwed in my right earring.

'I'm always careful,' I said, and managed to sound far brighter than I felt. Two hours at the house of someone who probably hated me was hardly my idea of time well spent. 'We can always leave if something doesn't feel right. I'll tell Tredwell to wait. Anyway, what can go wrong at a tea-party?'

'Remember the time you two were drugged at a a tea-room?'

'That was once!'

Albert came into the room and kissed me carefully on the cheek. 'You look lovely, Connie. Far too nice for a tea-party…'

His arms crept around my waist and I disentangled myself with some difficulty. 'I'm picking Katherine up in forty minutes, you know.'

He straightened up and stepped back. 'I'm surprised K's even going, what with all that rubbish in the newspapers.' I saw him watching me in the dressing-table mirror.

'Was there anything new today?' I had avoided the papers since coming across the twisted little snippet of gossip about James which had upset me so much. *If I refused to believe it*, I told myself, *then there was no point in looking.*

'Nothing of that nature, thank heavens.' Albert put his hands in his pockets. 'Did you know that Sir Richard Gresham's gone?'

An image of a stooped, heron-like man came into my head. Indeed, the newspaper cartoonists sometimes caricatured him as a bird. 'The MP? What do you mean, gone?'

'Stepped down with immediate effect. From both his ministerial position and his seat. There'll be a by-election, apparently.'

'How strange. He's been an MP ever since I can remember. And what a time to resign, with so much unrest over workers' rights.'

'Maybe it's worn him out,' said Albert. 'I mean, the reports of the debates go on for ever — imagine actually having to take part in them. He must be at least sixty.'

'Oh, look at the time! I must go and fetch Katherine.' I rose, and kissed him. 'I'd much rather stay and talk to you.'

He smiled. 'Try and enjoy it. I want a report of all the hats.'

'I'll do my best.'

***

'I don't think I've seen that lovely outfit before,' I said, as Katherine climbed up into the carriage wearing a mauve and black dress and a chic little hat.

'It is lovely, isn't it,' she said, and the corner of her mouth turned up a little. 'I thought I'd wear something new today.'

I studied Katherine for a moment but she clearly didn't intend to enlighten me. 'Are you looking forward to it?'

'I'm hoping we'll get a chance to speak to Alexandra alone,' she said. 'It depends how many people she's invited.' I had a sudden image of us in the middle of a tight throng of women, waving a hand at a distant Alexandra.

'What does our hostess look like?' I asked. 'I've never met her. Or if I have, I don't remember.'

'Brown hair, large eyes, pale, beautifully dressed, and very, very slender.' I resolved not to have more than two sandwiches and one cake. 'She'd blow away in a stiff breeze.'

'Oh. Oh dear.' My incipient jealousy of Alexandra Arrington vanished in a moment. 'Do you think she's unhappy?'

'I'm sure of it. She's upset about Toby, but that isn't all of it. I suspect this tea party is as much enjoyment as she's allowed to have.' Katherine's face took on a stony expression. 'Parents should consider the restrictions they place on their children's lives.' And she said no more until we pulled up in Park Lane.

***

135

Given Katherine's words, I had half-expected to encounter Alexandra Arrington either weeping beside a pond or propped up on a sofa. However, when we were announced she came forward to greet us, a tallish figure in a rose-patterned tea-gown which hung where it should have skimmed. 'How lovely to meet you at last, Mrs Lamont,' she said, with a shy smile. 'I have heard so much about you from Toby.' She leaned forward confidentially. 'I admired you from afar at the masked ball.'

'Oh!' I laughed, and hoped I didn't sound as self-conscious as I felt. 'That was all the work of my dressmaker and maid. As you can see, I'm much shorter in real life without six inches of piled-up hair.'

She made a little face. 'Someone complimented me on my candle costume, when I was meant to be a goddess.'

'The lights were dim, weren't they?' I said, trying to think of something better, but nothing came. 'What a beautiful room.' The drawing room was panelled below the dado with oak and above was rich green silk, with the armchairs and sofas upholstered in a slightly paler shade. The ceiling was high, the cornices beautifully moulded with a deep frieze of scrolls and flutes, and a sparkling chandelier lit the scene. It was beautiful but cold. Alexandra and her few guests looked lost in the middle of it.

'Come and have tea,' she said, and led Katherine and I to a vacant sofa. I remembered Albert's caution, and made sure that Alexandra poured out for all three of us before taking a sip.

Alexandra introduced the two other guests — a Miss

Phipps and a Miss Davies, one slim and one stout, who smiled politely, shook hands limply, and then went back to nibbling at their sandwiches. 'I also invited Miss Frobisher, but unfortunately she had a prior engagement.' She looked sorrowful, and I suspected that she doubted the existence of Maisie's prior engagement.

'Maisie is terrifically busy,' I said, taking a sandwich from the plate beside the nibblers. 'I feel as if I am on a waiting list to see her sometimes, and I've known her since we were fourteen.'

She brightened a little. 'Do you know Miss Frobisher, Mrs King?'

'A little,' said Katherine, choosing a poached chicken and lettuce sandwich. 'I've seen more of her in the last month or so.' She offered the plate to Alexandra, who made a gently dismissive gesture.

'Is that because of the balls?' said Alexandra, flushing a little. 'I saw her swan costume. What a wonderful night that was.'

'She made an excellent Hippolyta too,' I said, laughing. 'Did you spot her?'

Alexandra twisted her hands in her lap. 'I — I'm afraid I wasn't there.'

'Oh, what a shame,' said Katherine.

The twisting intensified unless it was almost a grinding motion. 'Would you care to see the paintings?' she said, rising abruptly. 'The Canaletto over the mantel is lovely.'

We rose with her, while the Misses Phipps and Davies sat side by side, chewing, their round eyes following us like a pair of rabbits. 'It's Venice at sunrise,' said Alexandra, loud enough to make me jump, as we stood in front of the painting. 'I wasn't invited,' she muttered. 'I knew I wouldn't be. Toby smuggled me into the first ball. I could only go because Mama had retired early and Father was at a presentation dinner. I read about the second ball in the *Tatler*. It sounded so magical.' Her eyes blurred with tears.

'It wasn't anything like as good as the first one,' I said. 'You really didn't miss much.'

'Who was there?' she breathed.

'It was hard to tell,' said Katherine. 'It was dark, as it was meant to be the enchanted forest, and of course everyone was masked and costumed.'

'That's true,' Alexandra said, reflectively. 'I only knew half the people because Toby pointed them out to me. Toby knows — knew everyone.'

'He was very popular,' I said, touching her arm, thin and hard beneath the silk of her dress.

She nodded. 'Yes. We sat out for a couple of dances together and he pointed out the Patchetts, and Miss Carroll and her fiancé, and Herbert Cresswell, and Miss Diana Lamington with her beau. Such fun! And I knew Miss Frobisher and Mr Bellairs, of course.'

'Ah, the swans.' I grinned.

'I didn't know that you knew Mr Bellairs,' said Katherine, a little teasingly.

Alexandra's eyes widened. 'Oh! Not in that way,' she said, as if Maisie might charge in at any moment. 'I saw him at court receptions sometimes. Father used to take me quite often, but — not so much now. Mr Bellairs — Archie — probably still goes with his father. It is such a

138

good opportunity for a young man.' Her expression softened. 'It was nice to see him having fun; he was always so serious and stern at the receptions.' Then she laughed, an unexpectedly musical sound. 'Oh, and do you know,' she said, turning to Katherine, 'you were right!'

Katherine looked puzzled. 'Was I?'

'Yes!' Again she lowered her voice. 'Lord Marchmont was at the ball!' She giggled. 'When I said "serious and stern" it must have jogged my memory. I had meant to tell you.'

'Good heavens,' said Katherine. 'Are you sure it was him?'

'Oh yes,' said Alexandra. 'He was standing there, very upright, in white tie and tails, and when Toby mentioned the All Hallows Orphanage, he nodded in that pompous way he has and muttered about a worthy cause and hoping the event would do it justice. But he only stayed until the dancing began. As soon as people started claiming their partners he stalked off, and I'm sure he said it was immoral.' Her smile was broad now. 'I think he was outraged. I don't care if he was, because he's always so strict and horrible. And rude, even at the receptions. I mean, Father and he are opposed politically, but there's no need to be —'

The door opened, and a tall man came in. 'I thought I heard voices,' he said, smiling.

'Father,' breathed Alexandra, and her face drained of colour.

'Are you having a nice tea party, dear?' He sat in an armchair. 'Won't you pour me a cup?'

'Of course.' Alexandra sat down and lifted the teapot.

'I hope you've eaten,' he said, and the stream of brown fluid wobbled into the cup.

'Yes, Father,' said Alexandra, to the teapot.

'Good.' He waited as the milk was added, and a cube of sugar. 'Tell me what you had for tea.'

The Misses Phipps and Davies hunched over their slices of seed-cake.

'I had a sandwich.'

He glanced at the plate. 'What sort of sandwich?'

'An — egg sandwich.'

'Was it a nice sandwich?'

She nodded.

He picked up the plate and held it out. 'Then you can eat another one, can't you?'

She hesitated, then took one and bit the corner off. It was a full minute before she swallowed.

'It is nice to see new people at home,' said Alexandra's father. 'My wife is an invalid, so we have to keep a quiet house, but a sober tea-party never did anyone any harm.' He twinkled, something I would have thought impossible. 'Mrs Lamont, isn't it? I sometimes bump into your husband in the City. Quite a coming man, I believe. We must invite you to dinner.' He turned to Katherine. 'And Mrs King. I couldn't place you at our last meeting, but your husband does such *brave* work.' He pressed her hand.

'I've finished,' said Alexandra, looking mutinous.

'Jolly good,' said her father. 'Have a piece of cake.'

A look of shocked despair came over her face, and she began to weep quietly.

140

'Oh dear,' said Alexandra's father. 'My daughter is overtired with the excitement of guests.' He rose, and we did too, and after a second Miss Phipps and Miss Davies joined us, with a slightly regretful glance at the cake plate. 'Do come again,' he said, with a smile. 'Phoebe will see you out.' And he sat back down.

It was an effort to wait until Tredwell had got the carriage underway.

'Did you *hear* that?'

'Did you *see* that?'

We stared at each other across the carriage.

'Come back to Marylebone,' I said. 'We need to talk this over.'

'We do,' said Katherine, 'but I have an appointment. I don't suppose you could drop me off in the Bayswater Road?'

I looked at her narrowly. 'Does James know?'

'I'm meeting James.' Again, that secret little look, then a giggle. 'I'll tell you afterwards.'

But I didn't really mind. I had more than enough to occupy me in the meantime.

Chapter 16
Katherine

James was waiting on the pavement as I alighted. As ever, my heart still skipped a beat when I saw him. His face was solemn until he spotted the carriage, and then his teasing grin reappeared as he doffed his hat and helped me down. 'When I said I wanted a baggage, Mrs Lamont, I meant something more substantial and less carroty.'

Connie giggled. 'Why Mr King, this is the best I could get for sixpence.' She waved like the Queen and the carriage rattled away.

'Rotters,' I said, tucking my arm in his. 'Shall we walk?' The day was fine but the roads busy.

'We'll walk home later,' said James. 'This is our cab. I'm sure it'll be marginally quicker and I'd rather not be late. How was tea?'

'It was . . . stilted,' I said as he handed me aboard. 'Poor Alexandra. Her father seemed worried about her but there was something —'

'Well, you did say he was over-protective.'

'Yes, he is. Most fathers are. Mine, of course, thinks on the one hand I should be home tatting, and on the other safe to leave for years while he gallivants. I doubt he'd notice if I didn't eat.'

'You don't. I've seen fatter sparrows.'

I shook my head. It was stifling in the cab but not as bad as the tube would have been, and in another sense not as bad as the Arringtons' drawing room. 'I don't eat a lot but I do eat and I enjoy it. Alexandra is starving herself. It's pitiful.'

'Mmm,' said James. His face was grim, then he caught my eye. 'But we have a job to do, Katherine. A secret mission.'

'And a nice one, for a change.'

'Indeed.' He smiled at last. 'Here we are.'

The street in Kensington was round the corner from James's Aunt Penelope's house, but it couldn't have been more different. The workhouse glowered over the roofs of small terraced houses. The children here were thin, and one or two were barefoot, but they were clean, as were the doorsteps they played on. A little church was tucked between the rows of houses.

'Here goes,' said James, helping me out of the cab and paying the driver.

Nathan was just inside the door with the rector and a young woman with blonde hair piled under a neat blue hat.

'Here they are,' said Nathan, and all three visibly relaxed.

'Everything is in order, then,' said the rector. 'Shall we

proceed?' He walked to the altar steps and waited.

It was hard not to recall my own wedding and feel sorry for Nathan's Sarah. My church had been full of guests and flowers, my family and friends delighted. Even Connie's wedding had involved her nearest and dearest. But Nathan and Sarah had only us as witnesses, a cousin whom Nathan barely knew and her husband. I was glad that I'd had time to arrange a bouquet for Sarah and extra flowers for the church, and had sent Nathan to Maria to see if she could help with a ready-made dress. Sarah was my height but full-busted despite her tiny waist. None of my clothes would fit her. But the bride looked lovely in a neat royal-blue outfit trimmed with white, her eyes shining as she shook my hand.

'You need someone to give you away, Miss Harper,' said James, and offered his arm. 'Katherine can be best woman. She may set a trend. Off you go, you two.' He waved me and Nathan up the aisle.

'I'm afraid we have no means of playing the wedding march,' said the rector as Nathan and I approached. 'Oh!'

We turned to see a small man in brown race down the aisle, career around the front pew and sit at the organ, catching his breath and then flexing his fingers. 'Arternoon vicar,' he said. 'The gentleman up there had a chat with me earlier and suggested a bit of extra practice.' He grinned. 'Perhaps I'll do some Mendelssohn, eh?'

Nathan was trembling beside me. He handed me a ring box and gave a weak smile. He looked back up the aisle to where James and Sarah stood and blinked hard several times.

'Marriage isn't that bad,' I joked, but he wasn't listening.

'She's lovely, isn't she?' he whispered.

'Yes,' I said.

As the music played, he whispered again. 'She deserves better than this, better than me.'

'It's you she wants, though,' I said. 'And everything will be fine.'

And here was Sarah, walking arm in arm with James to the Wedding March, her face alight.

'Who gives this woman to be married to this man?' intoned the rector.

'I do,' said James. He placed Sarah's hand into Nathan's and stood aside.

No one came in to object, there were no hymns, there were just the six of us in the little church. From outside came the sounds of children playing and people shouting, and the muffled noise of traffic from the main thoroughfare round the corner. The prayers and liturgy curled round us like an embrace and then they knelt for the final blessing before rising to share a shy kiss. The organist played as we signed the register, and when we left the church all felt beautiful and well. All that mattered to them was that they were married. Facing up to their parents could wait.

***

'It's ever so kind of you to give us a dinner,' said Sarah. She sat hand in hand with Nathan across the table from us, in the dining room of a Soho hotel run by Italians. We ate a light consommé, followed by a spaghetti alle vongole, pollo alla Romana and zabaglione. The wine, though only

James and I drank it, was light and summery.

'We're delighted to treat you,' said James. 'I thought somewhere quiet and intimate would be nicer than a fancy restaurant.'

'It's more than enough, especially after your help with the licence,' said Sarah. 'And Mrs King, how can I thank you for this dress? I can never repay you.'

'It's a gift,' I said. 'I know how much a nice dress can mean. It looks beautiful on you.'

'I chose something which will last,' said Sarah. 'But it's good to have pretty too.' She paused, fiddling with her napkin ring. 'Mr King, I'm ever such an admirer of yours. I've read your column for years. Not many rich people care enough to say what you say.'

'Some do,' said James.

'Yes, but you keep things in the papers which other people want kept quiet. You needn't, need you?'

'No. But I want to.' James took a sip of wine. 'Miss . . . Mrs Lawrenson, I know I've had an easy life. I can't do anything about that. Giving it all away and living like a pauper won't help anyone. Keeping in the same circle and telling people what's what just might.'

'Fair enough. Oh, and Nathan said you were interested in Mr Bellairs.'

James and I tried not to look at each other. 'We're interested in the talk he gave on Friday evening,' said James.

'He was very late,' said Sarah, picking up her spoon. 'Wasn't he, Nathan? Pa was ever so annoyed. "Typical toff, thinks we don't deserve the courtesy to be on time," he

146

said. Sorry Mr King, no offence intended.'

'None taken. How late was he?'

'Let's see. It was half past ten. Pa was about to give up. He didn't want to be lectured by a Bellairs again, but there you go. I think Lord Marchmont had set it up. He sets up a lot of talks by toffs.' Faint colour showed in her cheeks. 'Sorry.'

'Never mind,' said James. 'That's very interesting. But next time you want a toff to talk, come and ask me. I'll find you someone punctual.'

'Maybe you could talk yourself.'

'I'm not a speaker, but I might.'

Sarah smiled and ate a spoonful of zabaglione. Then she caught sight of Nathan's face and hers fell. He was staring into his dessert in despair.

'Now we've got to go home,' he said. 'If either of us have one. We've sent telegrams.' He swallowed and squeezed Sarah's hand. 'Mother will be furious. And so will your Pa.'

'Well…' Sarah put up her chin. 'We'll just have to face it and if we have to sleep under a hedge tonight, then so be it.'

'Nonsense,' said James. 'You needn't worry till tomorrow. The last part of your wedding present is that you're booked into this hotel for the night. We've put a bag of overnight things for you in the room.'

Nathan and Sarah went scarlet, then Nathan's eyes filled with tears and Sarah, bright cheeked, reached across the table to kiss my cheek.

'I'll come with you to speak to your parents tomorrow,'

I promised.

'We'll both come,' said James, rising. 'But now, we shall bid you goodnight and sweet dreams. Katherine turns into a pumpkin if she stays out too late, and with hair that colour she's halfway there. Come along Mrs King, we have quite a walk.'

***

'What's wrong?' I said, as we headed back to Bayswater.

'Why do you think something's wrong?' said James. 'It's a lovely evening. We've witnessed a wedding and sent two lovebirds off into married life. With any luck your Aunt Leah will be so irritated that she'll run away to sea and never be seen again. You're beautiful, I'm handsome and we know Archie Bellairs was late to his speaking engagement. If I could sing, I would — but I can't, so I shan't. It's my only fault. Aren't you pleased?'

'Stop it, James.' I brought him to a halt and studied his face. It was still early enough for the sky to be light. 'You can't hide from me. I know when something's wrong. Why did you say you'd come with me tomorrow to talk to their parents when you have an assignment?'

He sighed. 'Because I haven't an assignment,' he said. 'We're both out on our ear, Katherine. I'm sorry. The editor has said I must take a leave of absence until things die down. If they ever do.'

'Things? What things? That nonsense about the ball?'

'Oh, a bit of opium-eating wouldn't worry the editor. It's not as if it's illegal. But immorality is another thing, even though that's not illegal either.'

148

'Immorality? You?'

'Apparently so. The Lord Marchmont who foundered your career also invests in our paper. I never knew, but apparently he does. He has been complaining of the gossip published about me for days, but this was the final straw. I'm so sorry, Katherine, but you'd better see this.' James moved my arm so that he could reach his pocket. He handed me a cutting from a newspaper.

What can it mean when a baby-farmer hands the dark, curly-haired poppet of a recently deceased "lady" to the barren wife of a certain dark curly-haired do-gooder? How curious, since the do-gooder and the "lady" were once, apparently, engaged — and yet his old flame was living in destitution while he wallows in hedonism at masked balls. Perhaps he felt he could "own" his mistakes after all. I wonder where the poppet is now?

It took a while for the meaning to sink in. All the joy of the wedding vanished, and my face flamed. 'How could they? Surely it's libel!'

'No-one is named.'

'No, but — how could they publish such nonsense?'

'Do you really believe it's nonsense?'

I tore the paper into shreds, threw it into the gutter and put my hands on my hips. 'Are you mad? Of course I do! You and Geraldine? Not in a million years. And I'm not barren! I'm not! How could you think I'd believe this — this…?' I calmed down and took deep breath, then forced a smile and put my arms round him. I had known him long

149

enough to understand that when he stopped making jokes, he was at breaking point.

'Let's go home,' I said. 'Let's go home and go to bed. This is as low as it can get and it will pass. Everything passes. Tomorrow we'll start again.'

But when we got home Connie and Albert were waiting for us. James took Albert into his study to smoke, and Connie sat with me on the sofa. 'I had to talk to someone,' she said. Her face was drained of colour and her hands shaking. 'I've talked Albert to death. We don't know what to do. We visited my family home and found Mother so angry. She has been cut.'

'Oh no? How? Is she badly hurt?'

Connie studied the floor. 'I mean socially.'

It seemed such a small thing that I struggled not to snap at her. There must be more to it than there sounded. Connie would not be here otherwise.

'By whom?'

'Lady Marchmont,' said Connie. 'She absolutely refused to speak to Mother directly at a soirée and implied that she could not keep acquaintance with a woman who kept bad company.'

'Does she mean us?' The inference stung.

'I'm not sure,' said Connie. 'Mother wasn't certain if she meant the awful things in the press about James, or my attendance at the balls. Either way, she was mortified.'

'I'm so sorry.' I put my arm around her. Now was not the time to tell her the latest awful libel.

'Oh, Mother gave as good as she got, I think. But then she took it out on me, and I shouted at her and stormed out.' Connie sighed. 'How can we help Toby's father if we are both ostracised?'

'We can't just lie back and play dead,' I said. 'I won't have our names dragged through the mud when the worst any of us have done is wear silly clothes.'

The doorbell rang, and a moment later Susan came in with a telegram.

'The boy says he's to wait for an answer, mum,' she said.

I exchanged glances with Connie and opened it up.

Burglars STOP my room and nursery attacked STOP Engagement ring gone STOP Lucy unharmed but all her things gone STOP We are distraught STOP Alice Frampton.

CHAPTER 17
Connie

The telegram crumpled in Katherine's hand. 'Well, they do say bad things happen in threes,' she said, and began to laugh.

'What do you mean, threes? And why are you laughing? We need to go to your aunt!' Susan was still hovering a few feet away. 'Tell the boy that we'll come at once and not to worry.'

Katherine's laughs were more like hiccups now. 'Sorry,' she said. 'It's been a long day.'

'Go and pack an overnight bag,' I said. 'Aunt Alice and Lucy can stay at our house, and she'll feel better with you there too.'

Finally Katherine was quiet, and her breathing steady. 'Yes,' she said. 'Yes, you're right. I'll go and tell James. We'll all go.'

***

We wired Tredwell to get the carriage out, and took a

cab home, the four of us packed like sardines. Suddenly Mother's rage and bemusement, and my anger and embarrassment, were much smaller than they had been even an hour ago. I imagined Aunt Alice arriving home to find her house ransacked, and how I would feel if when we got home I found Bee asleep in a stripped room. But then that wouldn't happen, I reassured myself, because my jewellery box or the safe in the study would offer richer pickings for any thief —

'Katherine, why did you say bad things happened in threes earlier?'

She shot me a warning glance, which was difficult as we were sitting so close that we were practically cheek to cheek. 'You're not the only one who's had a bad day. I can't talk about it right now. Aunt Alice and Lucy are the priority.'

'Of course, but — I'm not being nosy. Well, I am, but I think it has something to do with the burglary.'

She looked inquiringly at James and he gave a small nod.

'James is on indefinite leave of absence because of all the rubbish in the papers,' she said. 'We heard today.' She shifted round to look out of the window.

'So James has been silenced, Albert and I are probably excluded from polite society, and little Lucy has had her belongings stolen.'

'Why would that be connected?' said Katherine, frowning. 'Lord Marchmont's dismissed James, effectively, and your mother's been cut at a party, but —'

'Connie may be right, Katherine.' James looked utterly

153

miserable. 'Perhaps some idiot has read the slurs in the paper and decided to punish that poor child for what they think I've done. How can I face your aunt?'

'Or…' Everyone looked at me. 'Give me a moment, let me think aloud. Lucy's a baby, she won't mind if her belongings are silver or not. But anyone who knew who her mother was would guess they'd be good quality. So either, again, someone is getting at you, or . . . or…'

'They've taken her things for another reason,' said Katherine. 'Probably to melt them down for the silver, or to pawn.'

'Maybe.' I sighed. The answer was on the tip of my tongue, but every jolt of the carriage seemed to shake it loose. For now, I resolved to keep my eyes open and my mouth shut.

***

Mina answered the door to us, looking tired and perturbed. 'Alice and Lucy are upstairs,' she said. 'We went out for dinner, as Mr Frampton is away on business, and when we got back, well —' She waved a hand behind her at the hall, which seemed just the same as usual.

'Is everything secure?' asked Albert. 'How did they get in?'

'They forced the nursery window. And no, it isn't. It's Horace and Mabel's day off, and they're not due until ten. We thought it could wait till then.'

'I don't think it can,' said Albert. 'I'll get Tredwell to sort something out.' He went outside.

'Has much been taken, Mina?' I asked.

Mina's expression turned to puzzlement. 'Not really. I

154

mean, Lucy's things are gone. Alice thought her engagement ring had been stolen, but then we found it in a different part of her jewellery box. They took a bead necklace that was on her dressing table, but left the silver candlesticks.'

'Maybe they heard a noise and cleared out,' said James.

'Maybe,' said Mina. 'It's just lucky that Hannah had taken Lucy downstairs to settle her. We found them curled up asleep on the sofa without an inkling of what had happened.' Her face darkened. 'Poor Hannah's beside herself, of course.'

'We'll go up,' said Katherine.

'I'll make tea,' said Mina.

Aunt Alice was sitting in the nursery armchair with Lucy in her arms and a guilty expression on her face, while the little nursemaid sobbed in the corner. 'I keep telling Hannah that it wasn't her fault,' she said. 'Perhaps she'll listen to you.'

'All her pretty things, the poor mite!' Hannah wailed. 'All her mother left her, but for her rattle!' We looked at Lucy, who regarded us solemnly, holding her rattle in an iron grip.

'At least she's got that,' I said. 'Hannah, can you pack some things for Mrs Frampton and Lucy and yourself? I think you'll be safest at our house for the night, and Lucy can go into the nursery with Bee.' Hannah wiped her eyes with her apron and scuttled away.

***

Aunt Alice, Lucy and Hannah journeyed with James and Katherine, driven by Tredwell, while Albert and I took a cab with Mina. 'You think it's odd too, don't you?' I said, as we bowled along the back roads.

'I do,' said Mina. 'But as James says, maybe they were disturbed before they had a chance to get to the other rooms. If they'd taken Andrew's picture, just for the silver frame —' I could imagine her fists clenching in the dark. 'And it's such an odd time to do it, when it's still quite light. Then again there's almost always a servant in, at least, and it's so rare for Alice and I to go out together in the evening nowadays.'

'They must have been watching the house,' I said. 'I don't think this was a chance attack.'

'But it would hardly be worth their while, when they could do so much better elsewhere,' Mina argued.

'No,' I said, and the next words came to me with no effort at all. 'They were looking for something, and they think they've got it.' And I added, to myself, *And Lord Marchmont is behind it, somehow.*

***

It took some time to get everyone settled to their satisfaction, and a great deal of running about by Nancy and Violet, but by half past eleven Albert and I had retired to bed. Katherine and James had both looked utterly exhausted, with dark shadows under their eyes, and I made a mental note to tell Nancy not to bring them tea till at least ten the next morning.

'Aunt Alice is a very light sleeper, you know,' I said, as Albert's arms encircled me.

'Just for once, Connie, at this time of day, I'm more interested in what's going on in your mind.'

I stiffened, then turned to look at him, which was completely pointless in the pitch-black room. 'Is it so obvious?'

'To me, yes.' I could tell he was smiling. 'I can almost hear the cogs whirring.'

'Cheek.' I smacked his side through the counterpane. 'What do you think, anyway?'

'I'm not sure,' he said. 'I don't understand why Lord Marchmont is so down on us, though. After all, it isn't as if we were the only people at the ball.'

'I want to expose him for the old hypocrite that he is,' I whispered, putting as much venom into the words as I could. 'I'd love to get him arrested and made to stand up in court, and then thrown into jail. Oh yes.' I rubbed my hands.

'But you can't get arrested for being a stuck-up prig.' I detected a distinct grin this time.

'That's what's wrong with the world,' I said, feeling most disgruntled. 'Lord Marchmont is cutting off his nose to spite his face by silencing James. They're on the same side, for heaven's sake! What does he think he's doing? They both want to defend workers and the poor!'

'Sssshh, you'll wake everyone if you shout like that.' Albert put a finger on my lips for a moment. 'If he's on the same side then he can't be behind all this, can he? He's a powerful man, an influential man, but someone has worked out how to manipulate him.'

'You're right,' I said, and kissed him. 'Have a merit mark, or a house point, or whatever it is you got at your school.'

157

'You're too kind,' Albert replied. 'I'd bow if I weren't lying down.'

'Sir Richard Gresham!' I whispered. 'Liberal MP, passionate about workers' rights, resigns without explanation. I wonder...'

'I doubt he went to the ball and got invited into the opium den,' said Albert. 'He doesn't strike me as a dancing man.'

'Perhaps one of his children did,' I said. I closed my eyes and tried to remember whom Alexandra had mentioned at her tea-party. Delia Carroll and her fiancé . . . that would be the Honourable Thomas Bebington, or 'The Hon Tom Beb' as we called him, son of Lord Bebington. 'Albert, remind me — which side of the house is Lord Bebington on?'

'He's a liberal,' said Albert, yawning. 'Votes with the party line.'

'And so is Lord Frobisher, Maisie's father.' I gasped. 'Oh good heavens above! And Archie Bellairs's father too!'

'So perhaps he was invited into the den to try and shame his father out of Parliament...'

'But then why would he come to the next ball, and lure James in?'

Somewhere in Marylebone, a church clock chimed midnight.

'I don't think you'll solve that one tonight,' said Albert. 'I have an early meeting, and I need my beauty sleep even if you don't.' He gave me a final squeeze and turned over. 'Goodnight, Connie. Sleep well.'

I didn't, of course. I lay awake, Alexandra's guest list

floating through my mind, her high, reedy voice reciting it as I tried to piece it together, and Archie Bellairs ran through my dreams, pursued by Lord Marchmont in an ass's head, until a cab driven by Geraldine ran Archie down and Lucy bashed him with her rattle. Maisie applauded from the sidelines. 'Wasn't that fun?' she asked, her eyes sparkling through her mask.

But I couldn't answer. I was wearing the ass's head and as loud as I shouted, no one could hear. I turned to Katherine and James, but they had been gagged with mask ribbons and their eyes stared at me pleadingly above the bright show. Alexandra was still going through the guest list, but her father appeared and fed her sandwich after sandwich, cramming food in till her cheeks bulged and she had to cover her mouth —

I was shaken awake. 'You were having a bad dream, darling,' said Albert, looking worried. Cold grey light stretched its fingers around the curtains. 'I'm sorry to wake you, but you were making funny noises. And you sounded upset.'

I blinked. 'I was,' I said. 'And it was a nightmare.' When I rubbed my eyes, my face was wet. 'But I'm awake now.'

CHAPTER 18
Katherine

I was unsurprised to find Aunt Alice in the nursery early next morning. She was getting in the way of Hannah and Nanny as they fed the babies, who were were themselves making things more difficult by putting their hands up at the wrong moments, grabbing spoons and prodding their unappetising breakfast.

'Are you sure she's not too upset to eat gruel? Should she have a nap? Do you think she has a fever?'

Nanny was steering her towards the door as I arrived.

'Everything is as it should be, Mrs Frampton. Little Lucy is unaware that anything is amiss. It's a blessing to see a little rosiness in her cheek. It may be another tooth, but I think it is happiness.' She virtually pushed Aunt Alice into my arms. 'Here is Mrs King. She'll take you to have your own breakfast, I'm sure.'

The door shut firmly behind us, we went to the dining room and looked in the chafing dishes for the best that Mrs

Jones had to offer. I had a sudden urge for gruel. James joined us a few moments later, nonchalant as ever, and made a joke likening the bacon to fossilised leaves. Only the circles under his eyes betrayed his inner distress.

'Aunt Alice,' I said as I poured her coffee, 'from what Nancy said, I think Connie wanted us to lie in. Please would you tell her we had to leave early to keep a promise and I'll be back as soon as I can. Probably lunch time.' I looked at the devilled lobster and puréed brains on my plate. After the rich food of the previous night, I yearned for plain fare. 'Or no, perhaps before lunch. She and I shall eat at an old haunt, and then Mrs Jones needn't bother to cook on our behalf. Please don't worry.' I reached for her hand. 'Albert will be down soon, and he'll help with the police enquiries until Uncle Donald comes home, but James and I can't stay just now.'

Half an hour later, we collected Nathan and Sarah from the little hotel. It was good to see that of all the emotions struggling for the upper hand on their faces, a secret joy was winning.

***

Sarah's father stood in his printing shop, arms crossed, glaring at Nathan as if he was trying to ignite him. A little redness about his eyes suggested that he was more upset than angry. The small room was neat and well-lit, smelling of ink and clean paper. The two assistants had been sent for a break.

'I-I'm s-sorry, Mr Harper,' stammered Nathan, 'but we couldn't bear to be apart any longer.'

'That's all well and good,' said Mr Harper. 'But how

are you going to support her, working as some sort of stooge for a head-in-the-clouds storyteller who gets lost in foreign climes?'

'M-Mr Demeray is Mrs King's father, Mr Harper.'

Sarah's father uncrossed his arms in conciliation. 'I'm very sorry, madam. No offence was intended but —'

I couldn't help myself from bursting into laughter. 'Don't worry, Mr Harper, it's the best description of Father I've heard in years.'

Some of the tension left the room. 'You can see my difficulty, Mrs King,' Mr Harper said, lighting his pipe. 'We're a hard-working family. I didn't raise Sarah to sit back waiting for a man to keep her, I trained her. Look at the ink on her fingers. It's not usual, but Harper and Daughter I was going to call this business now she's twenty-one. Now what do I do? I don't mean to be rude, but I don't suppose you understand about earning a living and —'

'Mrs King used to work in an office, Pa,' said Sarah. 'She knows what it's like to feel pride in your work. Nathan says she hardly ever sits still. And this is Mr King from the *Chronicle*. You know how you admire him.'

Nathan swallowed. 'Please give us your blessing, Mr Harper. I promise to take good care of Sarah and if she wants to keep working here then . . . well, that's up to her.' Sarah squeezed his arm. 'I'll explain to Mother. I love working for my uncle and even if it's not a large salary, it's something. And if he'll let us, hopefully we can live in his house in Fulham for the time being.'

Sarah's face dropped.

'Well it'll have to be that or live in the printing room, ducks,' said Mr Harper to her. 'There's no room at home. Well, young man.' He reached out his hand. 'Welcome to the family. But if you ever raise a hand to her I'll put your head in the printing press and see what happens.'

**

'How delightfully romantic!' exclaimed Father, shaking Sarah's hand until I feared it would fall off. 'How marvellous! And a printer to boot — how useful! How much do you charge for printing books? I've never met elopers before. It's wonderful, isn't it Leah?'

If Aunt Leah's face could have closed any further it would have been concave. Her eyes had narrowed into currants and her lip curled as she surveyed Sarah from head to toe.

'Won't you welcome your daughter-in-law?' I said. The two women stared into each other's faces. Despite my aunt's glare, Sarah did not quail. She stood straight and lifted her head and did not blink.

'Good morning, Mrs Lawrenson,' she said. 'I promise to make your son happy.'

Aunt Leah made a noise reminiscent of a cat. Then she rounded on me and James. 'This is your doing,' she said. 'You and your lack of morals. Don't think I haven't seen what's in the papers. You have encouraged my son to turn against me and now he's married a mere shop girl with ideas above her station. I knew it was a mistake becoming embroiled in this family again. My dear late husband is spinning in his grave.'

'Come now, Leah,' said Father. 'Whatever are you

talking about?'

'I am leaving,' said Aunt Leah. 'I cannot stay in a house where fatherless babies and common girls are welcomed. I have nowhere I may go, but I shall leave immediately.' She uncurled her lip enough to wobble it and turned dry eyes on her son.

Nathan made a tiny movement towards her but I stood on his foot. Sarah gripped his arm.

'I'm sorry if you are upset, Mother,' he said. 'But I can't have my wife treated with disrespect.'

'Shall I help you pack, Aunt?' I said.

'Humph,' said Aunt Leah. 'I am going to my room. Tell Ada to bring my meals there for the foreseeable future.' She slammed out of the room.

'She'll be sorry,' murmured James. 'I dread to think what Ada will do to the food if she has to lug it upstairs.'

I gave Sarah a hug. 'I've wired Margaret,' I whispered. 'She'll come back, if only to watch the fireworks. But she'll be on your side. Don't worry. You can always come to us if things get difficult.'

'That's all right, Mrs King,' murmured Sarah with a tiny wink. 'I've dealt with worse than Mrs L. I'm quite looking forward to it.' She studied me more closely. 'But if you don't mind me saying so, you look all in. I hope you're going home for a rest.'

'Not yet,' I whispered back, my good humour dissolving. 'I have something else to do.'

***

Lord Marchmont's London residence was surprisingly small. I handed in my card and waited in the vestibule. The space was austere to the point of emptiness. There was barely a painting on the wall and, apart from the dish for cards, the side table bore one small glass dome full of wax flowers.

As I studied a seascape a small cough made me jump. 'His Lordship says he will see you,' intoned a footman.

I followed him into a warm, dark study, thick with the aromas of leather and tobacco. Lord Marchmont sat behind a mahogany desk, papers spread before him, and rose as I entered. A secretary waited to one side, appraising me through round spectacles and making me feel like a beetle under a microscope. After a brief, wordless pause in which Lord Marchmont gestured towards a chair, a well-dressed woman entered the room through another door and sat on the far side of the hearth. When we were both settled, Lord Marchmont resumed his seat.

'Good morning, Mrs King,' he said. 'This is an unusual hour to call.'

'Thank you for seeing me, my lord,' I said. 'I appreciate that you are busy.'

'I am indeed very busy. The country is going to the dogs. However perhaps I owe you an audience, and here is my dear wife to be a chaperone for you, since you have not brought one.' He frowned. 'I am not sure if this indicates a free spirit or laxness of conduct. Or perhaps your husband and father care little for your reputation.'

I gritted my teeth. 'My father and my husband trust me to make them proud. I am quite respectable, Lord Marchmont. That is why I am here, to plead my case. If it is necessary to have a male escort in Mayfair in 1893 in broad daylight, I shall feel that the country has indeed "gone to the dogs". I worked hard for Queen and country to bring traitors to account. I don't believe that my record is in any way blemished and —'

'No, indeed,' said Lord Marchmont. 'You were an asset, despite the fact that women do not have the mental capacity to understand the complexity of politics, espionage or economics. Do they, dear?' He smiled at his wife, who simpered at him and gave me a look so malevolent it was all I could do to keep a neutral expression. 'I'm sure you were very lucky with your guesses.'

'My lord…'

'The problem is, my dear Mrs King, that though from what I gather your intentions are good, you have fallen into bad company.'

'Me?'

'Dear me, mixing with typists has made you terribly ungrammatical.' Lord Marchmont allowed himself a dry laugh. Then his face closed into seriousness. 'Your husband is one of the gentry, I understand. Presumably that is how you were invited to that deplorable ball. Dancing is at least frivolous and at worst, sinful. All that proximity, the rhythm, the… At any rate, that would have been bad enough. But then it became clear to me that there was intoxication, gambling, debauchery. Quite why you didn't marry a quiet suburban gentleman of independent means who —'

'James is passionate about his work, my lord,' I interrupted. 'He cares deeply about social injustice, as you do. He does everything in his power to use his advantage to help others.'

'That's as may be.' Lord Marchmont leaned forward. 'But he is a sinner.'

'He isn't!'

'We have all sinned and fallen short of the glory of God.'

'Yes, my lord. Of course we have. We all have.' I took a breath. 'But he is no more sinful than I, or, I'm sure, than you.'

There was a sharp intake of breath from both Lady Marchmont and the secretary. Lord Marchmont frankly glared. 'You are living proof, Mrs King, of why I refuse to support women's franchise,' he said. 'You have clearly not the brains to understand when something is beyond the pale. I will not have my department, as long as I am minister for it, debased by association with an adulterer and an opium-eater.'

'But James is neither!' I cried. 'All he wants is for everyone to have a fair chance. Nothing else. Isn't that what your party wants?'

'My party wants stability, Mrs King. The Empire depends on stability. Fair chances are one thing; stability is another. I will not have anyone rocking the boat. If someone does, then I will expose him as the degenerate he is by whatever means it takes. Good day, Mrs King. My man will see you out.'

CHAPTER 19
Connie

As it turned out I was the one who slept in. I woke at Nancy's knock to a room blazing with light. Albert's side of the bed was empty. 'What time is it?' I groaned.

'A quarter to ten, ma'am,' said Nancy. 'The master said to let you sleep as you'd had a bad night. He's gone out to one of his meetings.' She smiled a little indulgently.

I blinked. 'I meant to ask you to let the Kings sleep in.'

Nancy grinned. 'No chance of that, ma'am, they were both up and out by half past eight. Mrs King said to say she'd see you for lunch. I think she means at a restaurant.'

'Oh. Um, thank you.'

'Shall I send Violet, ma'am?'

'Perhaps in fifteen minutes.'

Alone in the big bed, I poured myself a cup of tea and tried to remember my whispered conversation with Albert in the middle of last night, although my strange dream kept intruding and making me laugh. And yet — oh, if only

168

Katherine were here!

Barely a minute seemed to have passed before Violet's timid tap. 'Nancy said I was to come to you, ma'am,' she said, her eyes sliding to the wardrobe. 'What are your plans for today?'

'Apart from being told that I'm going to a restaurant with Mrs King, I have no idea.' Violet waited patiently as I marshalled my thoughts, cup in hand. 'Oh! I know. Could you go to the library and find a book called *Debrett's Peerage*, and bring it to me, please?'

Violet opened her eyes very wide. 'A book?'

'Yes, a book. *Debrett's Peerage*. It's red.'

Violet bobbed. 'A red book,' she murmured. '*Debrett's Peerage*.'

I poured another cup of tea and settled against my pillows, prepared for a long wait. I could not decide whether my mother would have been more shocked or more proud that we owned a copy of the book, or that I was consulting it, though for different purposes than hers. Then again, Mother and I were not on speaking terms at present. I winced at the memory of my mother, nose in the air, declaring grandly, 'You are a married woman now, Constance, and I, thank God, am no longer responsible for your actions. However, your low behaviour is affecting the prospects of this family, and I shall not be associated with it.' I could imagine the humiliation she had been subjected to, and if Albert had not accompanied me I suspected that I would have been dealt with rather more severely.

To my surprise Violet returned within ten minutes, book in hand. 'Will you get ready now, ma'am?' she asked, hopefully.

I was already leafing through the pages. 'Oh, could you bring me up a breakfast tray, please? Just toast, and bacon, oh and scrambled eggs if Mrs Jones has made any.'

'Yes, ma'am.' I could have been mistaken, but I thought I saw Violet roll her eyes as she left the room.

'There,' I whispered as I found the entry. *GRESHAM, Sir Richard.* I skipped past his education and honours — those were for another time — to *Issue. Sons living: Richard (b. 1868), Edward (b. 1870), Thomas (b.1873).* I crossed to the bureau and noted them down, along with a daughter, Amelia. The sons, though, would be my focus. They would probably have gone to court events with their father. Alexandra would have seen them there; and if one of them had attended the ball, she might remember.

Alexandra... I turned to the beginning of the book. *ARRINGTON, Sir Joshua.* The baronetcy had been created in Tudor times. *Married Frances, daughter of 2nd Lord Hetherington, 1863. Daughters living — Alexandra.* That, apart from their residence and a description of their coat of arms, was about it. Alexandra was the end of the Arrington line, and I sensed the pressure which had been put on her to marry well, or perhaps find a husband willing to take the Arrington name and keep it alive. But all Alexandra wanted was Toby...

I closed the book with a decisive thud as Violet entered with my tray. 'Ooh, lovely,' I said, lifting the cloche to reveal an appetising plateful. 'I shall wear my midnight-blue silk this morning, Violet.'

Violet looked astonished. 'For lunch with Mrs King?'

170

I smiled. 'I intend to pay a call first.'

***

'Shall I stay, ma'am?' asked Tredwell.

'Yes please,' I said, hoping rather guiltily that he would have a good long wait.

I had played the scene in my head at least ten times on the journey to Mayfair; handing in my card, being received by a delighted Alexandra, a cosy chat over tea during which, with careful probing, she would say that yes, she had seen Richard or Edward or Thomas Gresham at the ball, and yes they had disappeared at some point, and would I like more tea?

Phoebe answered the door and I handed in my card, with the top-left corner folded down. 'I was passing and thought I would call to thank Miss Arrington for her lovely tea party,' I said, as blandly and grandly as I could.

Phoebe eyed the carriage. 'I'll go and ask, ma'am.'

She came back two minutes later. 'I'm afraid Miss Arrington is a little unwell today, ma'am.'

'Oh, what a shame,' I said. 'In that case, please can you send Miss Arrington my best wishes for a speedy recovery, and I hope to see her in the best of health very soon.' Phoebe nodded, and the door closed.

I got into the carriage in a fine grump. 'Home, ma'am?' asked Tredwell.

I lifted my chin. I would not be defeated. 'Not yet. Drive me to Miss Frobisher's, please.'

And Maisie was not at home, either.

'I give up,' I said, throwing myself into the corner of the carriage and folding my arms with complete disregard for my poor dress. 'Home please, Tredwell.'

***

Katherine finally arrived at our house at a quarter to two. I had foregone lunch, since Nancy had mentioned a restaurant, and stayed in my blue silk for the same reason. 'So where are you taking me?' I asked, doing my best to smile even though I was cross at her lateness.

Katherine looked dazed.

'For lunch?' I said. 'Nancy passed on your message.'

'Oh.' Katherine studied the floor. 'I'm sorry. Of course. How awful of me. I forgot. I just called to get our things but yes, of course, lunch…'

'Well, thank you very much,' I said. 'Never mind that you sneaked off without saying goodbye, and I've missed lunch because of you!' I flounced to the staircase.

'Where are you going?' called Katherine. I was already on my way upstairs. 'We can still go somewhere.'

'I'm going to take this stupid dress off and go to the nursery. I should have been there this morning, except I was too busy being cut by half my acquaintance and waiting for you to show up.'

'Connie, wait —'

'I've waited long enough,' I said, rather loudly, as I carried on upstairs. 'Nancy can get your things.'

'Connie, I'm sorry, I didn't think —' Katherine's feet were pattering upstairs behind me, and I quickened my step to reach my boudoir door.

'No. You didn't.' I stepped in, and closed the door.

Stupid dress, I muttered, as I undid the fastenings. *Stupid day*. Katherine didn't care about Toby's death, not

172

in the way that I did. She was too busy dealing with her own problems, which was understandable, but her disregard for me still hurt.

'I'm still here,' called Katherine.

'I'm busy,' I snapped. 'Go away and pack, since you're so keen to leave.' My dress fell to the floor and I stepped out of it. I was tempted to leave it where it was, but the thought of Violet's disapproval made me lay it on the bed.

'Please listen. I thought I had time to see Lord Marchmont before I came back,' said Katherine, her voice muffled by the door. 'But everything took longer than I expected and he wouldn't listen to a word I said.' I heard her voice change in the way it did when she was forcing herself not to cry. 'It was awful. He patronised me. And then I wanted to curl up and hide. I'm so sorry Connie, I didn't mean to…'

'Oh, for heaven's sake!' I flung open the door and yanked Katherine inside. Angry as I was, I couldn't leave her to sob on the landing. 'Sit down.' I reached into the wardrobe for a wrap and put it on, then turned to Katherine, who looked very small in the armchair, and utterly drained. 'I wish you'd shout back at me,' I said, all my ire dissolved in an instant. 'That would be much easier.'

Katherine looked stricken. 'I can't,' she said, gripping the arms of the chair. 'I'm too sad, and too tired. It's such a waste. Lord Marchmont won't give James his job back, or let the Department take me back either.'

I crouched next to her. 'He probably won't right now, but I think I'm starting to understand why.'

173

'Oh, I understand exactly,' said Katherine, and I pitied the arms of the chair. 'Any appearance of immorality must be suppressed.'

'No, but listen —' And I poured out my conversation with Albert last night, and my research in *Debrett's* this morning.

Katherine listened, and gradually the colour returned to her face, and her grip on the chair relaxed. 'That makes sense,' she said at last, patting my hand. 'But he won't listen to a pair of women.'

'Then we shall find a way to make him listen,' I said, and rang the bell. 'Are you sure you can't manage some food?'

***

Katherine picked her way through poached eggs on toast, while I tackled cold beef and pickles and felt much better for it. 'I can't think on an empty stomach,' I said at last, laying down my knife and fork.

'You still don't want to involve the police?' asked Katherine.

I considered, and shook my head. 'Not if I can help it,' I said. 'Or at least, if there's a way that can avoid a public trial. Certainly as far as Toby is concerned.'

'I just —' Katherine wiped her mouth. 'What you said sounds completely plausible, but how shall we get any of these people to admit what happened? The whole point is that the victims will want it kept quiet.'

'That's the horrible, cunning nature of it,' I said. 'But I shall not give up. Not for you, or James, or Toby, or Sir Richard Gresham, or all the others.' I rang for Nancy to

174

clear away. 'I'll get a dress on and then we can go to the nursery. Aunt Alice is still fussing just as much, I'm sure, and Nanny will need a break. I know I would.'

We found Bee and Lucy being prepared for an outing, while Aunt Alice stood by with a shawl. 'But will they be safe in the same perambulator?' she said, in distressed tones. 'What if, completely by accident of course, one pushed the other out?'

'One at each end, ma'am,' said Nanny, bending to retrieve a stray bootee and put it on a waving pink foot. Bee giggled and, as Nanny came into view, dropped her rattle on the floor. Nanny bent again. 'Oh you silly girl, look what you've done!' She showed me the two pieces of the rattle — the ivory handle and the silver body. 'Oh, what a shame…'

I took the pieces and examined them. 'It's all right, it isn't broken. Look, the rattle screws back tog —'

'Wait.' Katherine put her hand on mine. 'There's something in the handle.' She took it from me and, holding it close to her face, tried to prise it out.

'There can't be,' I said. 'I never even knew it came apart. Did you know when you bought it?'

'I didn't buy it,' said Katherine. 'We need tweezers.'

'Shall I get some, ma'am?' asked Nanny.

'There's a pair on my dressing-table,' I said. 'Of course you bought it, Katherine. It was your christening gift, remember?'

'I bought Bee a rattle,' said Katherine, 'but not *this* rattle. Do you see the chip on that part? This is Lucy's rattle.'

'Here you are, ma'am,' said Nanny, handing the tweezers to Katherine, who screwed her face up as she picked at the handle.

'Got it,' she said finally, extracting a long quill of rolled paper. She unrolled it, scanned it, and handed it to me. 'We might just have what we need.'

Chapter 20
Katherine

I watched as Connie's eyes widened. She lowered the paper and stared at me, then her eyes twinkled and a grin spread over her face.

'Shall we rise to the challenge, Miss Fleet?' I said.

'We shall, Miss Caster.'

I burst out laughing and flung my arms round her. Bee, with no idea what was making me happy, started giggling and then so did Lucy. It was the first time any of us had heard her make any sort of definite sound. Her delighted chuckling made everyone else join in. Even Aunt Alice stopped fussing to swoop Lucy up and kiss her. The shawl dropped to the floor and Nanny whisked it out of sight.

'Come along, Connie,' I said. 'Let's leave the nursery outing be. I owe you more than one apology, but more importantly, I owe you a meal. There's still just about time to visit a certain tea-shop. I believe they have a French pastry chef working for them now.' I reconstructed the rattle for Lucy but kept the paper in my hand.

'We need to keep it hidden,' whispered Connie. 'Follow me.' She rose, kissed Bee and we went arm in arm to her morning room.

'Not the safe?' I asked.

'Too obvious,' she said. Scanning the room to make sure none of the servants were there, she lifted down an old daguerreotype of an irritable-looking woman in a hideous black bonnet like a monstrous crow mantling her head. 'Grandmama Swift,' Connie explained. 'I've hidden things behind the old dragon for years: diaries, Albert's love letters... No-one would ever take her down for a closer look. One of Mother's maids wouldn't even dust her for fear of the evil eye. I said I liked to be reminded of her and brought it with me. She and Mother couldn't bear each other, so there were no objections.' She ran her nail along the gummed strip that fastened the backing to the frame and revealed a tiny slit, into which she slipped Geraldine's note. 'There you are Grandmama, something to read.' She resealed the gap and hung the picture, then looked at me. 'What's the matter?'

'Albert wrote love letters?'

Connie went pink and giggled. 'Didn't James?'

We went into the vestibule to collect our outdoor things. The nursery party could be heard coming from the third floor. Before she could get distracted I led Connie to the front door and we stepped down to the carriage.

'Well,' she said, 'didn't he?'

'He sent me a poem once.' It was my turn to blush. I had a lot to tell Connie but wasn't sure I was ready to

178

disclose a ditty which had gone: *My darling isn't very tall and her hair is purest carrot. She spends her days in the music-hall and dresses like a parrot. She scowls a lot and kicks my shins, but I love her more than anything.* 'I can't quite recall it.'

'Come on, Katherine,' said Connie. 'You've bottled things up for so long that you're like a magnum of champagne about to explode. What is it?'

Where to start?

'It's been a few months, and today was probably the final straw,' I said eventually. 'I always forget that I don't have to struggle on alone. I hadn't even told James half of it.'

We had arrived at the tea-shop by the time I finished, starting with how I felt about trailing round with Father on his tours, Margaret leaving home, the mixed blessing of Aunt Leah deciding to reconcile with us on her husband's death, the lack of confidence I'd sometimes felt undertaking Mr Maynard's assignments alone, and the pregnancies that had perhaps never existed outside my own imagination.

'I wish you'd said.' Connie reached over and held my hands.

'I didn't want to make you feel under pressure to come back.'

'I didn't mean that,' she said. 'I meant the other thing.'

'It was all so nebulous,' I explained as we were handed to the pavement. 'And I didn't want to distress you over nothing.'

'I was worried my having Bee was making you sad. I'm

not silly. I know you want a child.'

'Oh, but —' I put my hands to my mouth. 'No, you've got it all wrong. I didn't mind about you and Bee! I minded about all those poor neglected children. The ones dying in the workhouses and slums, or the one whose parents didn't care or didn't want them.'

'If you're sure,' said Connie. 'That makes me feel so much better.'

'We've had so little time to talk recently,' I said. 'It's felt wrong.'

'I agree. And now there's no time to waste on misunderstandings.'

We stopped talking as we were escorted to a table near the window and handed menus.

'Where do we start?' I said.

'Well, I was thinking with Darjeeling and a choux…'

'I meant with, shall we say, *Grandmama's secret*.'

'Ah yes.' Connie extracted a small notebook and pencil from her bag. I had learnt to read upside down but her notes looked like utter gibberish.

'If you can do shorthand, so can I,' she said, catching my expression. 'What are you grinning at?'

'Something Mr Maynard said before he showed me the door.'

Connie held my gaze. 'Do you think he can help?'

'Maybe,' I said. 'But I'd rather we did this alone. Especially given what you've discovered. If I could get into the Department and look at files that would be one thing, but I don't want to compromise him. Besides, I'd rather we managed on our own like we did before.'

Connie added some scribble to the page. Her face was shining. A shadow fell over the table and we both looked up expecting the waitress and perhaps the sweet trolley, but to our surprise it was Connie's sister Veronica with a friend in tow. The friend turned to seek out the waitress and secure a table.

'Hullo Katherine,' said Veronica. 'Connie, Father let me telephone to your place but you'd just left. Nancy said I'd find you here. I think Mother is being utterly unreasonable. And I don't think you're the only one to have been maligned. I saw Maisie Frobisher earlier and she looked quite woebegone. Have you eaten? Are you going? There isn't another table free and I do so need to get away from Mother…'

'Oh for goodness' sake,' said Connie, forcing her things into her bag with such force the pencil snapped. 'Take our table. We have visits to make.' She heaved a huge sigh as the waitress bore down on us with a trolley holding all manner of delights. 'I despair,' she continued in bitter tones. 'I don't think I'll ever have a decent meal today.'

***

I didn't know Maisie well — she was more Connie's friend than mine — but I knew her well enough to be able to see what Veronica meant. Gone was the teasing, frivolous air, replaced by a look of low despair. Connie was evidently nonplussed. She had half-expected to be turned away again, but we had been ushered by Maisie's footman into her panelled study where she sat behind a large escritoire, chewing the end of a pen like a schoolgirl.

It seemed less than five minutes since I'd been carpeted

181

in Lord Marchmont's study. As Connie and I sat on the Chesterfield, the smell of leather and tobacco brought back enough of my fury to make my face burn anew.

Maisie was very modern and lived in a townhouse left to her by a grandfather. The study, while feminine with warm colours and pretty ornaments, was nevertheless very much a working place. The books, old and new, mostly consisted of travel diaries, maps and foreign texts and were disorganised, as if she read several of them at a time. It was hard to reconcile this side of her with the drawling socialite portrayed in the illustrated press, dancing in marvellous dresses at the most fashionable events.

Maisie must have seen me wrinkle my nose, for she waved her hand at an ashtray. 'I've taken up smoking. They say it's quite the latest thing for ladies.' The smile on her face did not match her wary eyes.

'Really?' said Connie. 'Do show me how. Perhaps I might try it.'

I stared at her. 'Connie —' What on earth would Albert say if I let her smoke? On the other hand, the idea of attempting to stop her made me boggle.

Maisie swallowed. 'I've run out of cigarettes.'

'Oh. I thought that was pipe ash,' said Connie.

Maisie stood up, walked to the window and looked out. The walled garden was warm with afternoon sun and she was silhouetted against it, her normally straight-backed frame slumped, her hands fiddling with the pen she hadn't put down.

Connie was rising to go to her when Maisie straightened and turned back to us. Her face displayed its normal nonchalant sociability.

'I'm so sorry,' she said. 'I am being unspeakably rude. We'll take tea.' She rang for the maid, gave instruction and sat in the armchair opposite the Chesterfield. 'Actually, Mrs King, I have been meaning to write to you. I'm sure you're aware that I have had my share of scurrilous gossip in my time. Nothing I do is worse than anything the average gentleman does, yet apparently it makes me shocking. I'd like you to know that I feel for you and your husband very much. Hopefully I don't need to tell you that I refuse to read anything about him, or to believe what I have heard, but it will pass. It will.'

'Thank you,' I said. 'That means a great deal.'

I looked at Connie. It was such a kind thing to say, and now we were going to say something which would hurt her.

'Miss Frobisher,' I said, 'we're here with some bad news of our own.'

Maisie's smile faltered. 'Indeed?'

'It's about Archie,' said Connie.

'A-Archie? I haven't seen him since the Midsummer Night's Ball.'

'Yes, Archie,' Connie replied. 'I'm glad you haven't seen him. I'm afraid he's…' She glanced sideways at me and I gave the smallest nod I could. 'He's a wanted man. On the night of that ball, he tried to give — James opium. He may have taken some himself.' She glanced at me again. 'Then a few hours later, after he'd left the Beaulieu, Geraldine Timpson died.'

Maisie's mouth dropped open. She went pale, then

frowned. 'But that was an accidental death. The inquest found she took too much laudanum. What had that to do with Archie?'

'He was one of the last people to see her,' I said.

'No, no, he left early to give a speech!' Maisie said. 'He told m —' She fell silent, forcing another smile.

Connie shook her head. 'I thought you hadn't seen him,' she said. 'There is over an hour unaccounted for between when he left the ball and when he arrived to give the speech. I'm afraid he looks very guilty.'

There was a small thump.

'Oh, that maid,' said Maisie, eyeing the door. 'She's forever knocking into things.'

'That wasn't outside the room,' said Connie. 'Tell me, Maisie, is this the room where we used to play when your grandfather was alive?' She walked over to the fireplace and stared at the carved roses in the panelling.

Maisie slumped, straightened, then gave a tiny, resigned laugh. 'It is. You always did have a wonderful memory.'

Connie gave her a gentle smile and then pressed one of the roses. A portion of panelling moved outwards and Archie Bellairs fell at her feet.

'It wasn't me!' he said. 'It wasn't. You have to believe me. I'll tell you everything — everything. But you have to protect me. I don't want to end up like Langlands or Geraldine. I want to live! I want to live!'

CHAPTER 21
Connie

Archie Bellairs was true to his word — and those words poured out of him like water. I had to ask him to pause several times while I noted the key points. The only significant hiatus was when the maid brought the tea in, and, I noted, showed no surprise at Archie's presence in the room. Once she had left I raised an eyebrow at Maisie. 'How long has Mr Bellairs been here?'

Maisie's eyes clouded, then she lifted her chin. 'Since the day after the ball. You can make what you like of it.' Her eyes flashed. 'But if I had known what — what sort of *worm* I was dealing with, I assure you that he would never have set foot in the house.' She looked across the desk at Archie, and I was surprised that he did not turn to stone then and there. 'I could box your ears with pleasure —'

'There's a long queue, Maisie,' said Katherine.

Maisie's mouth twitched. 'But handing him over to the police is a better punishment —'

'No!' cried Katherine, Archie and I, all at the same time.

Maisie's finger touched the button of the bell. 'No?' A little smile lit her eyes.

'No! Please, I implore you!' Archie fell to his knees at her feet.

'Stop that at once,' snapped Maisie, her lip curling. Then she looked at us, and her face was dangerously calm. 'Why not?'

'There are several reasons,' I said. 'First of all, I made a promise to someone not to involve the police. Secondly, we can pull the net tighter more quickly if we act without police involvement until the last minute. And thirdly —'

'Thirdly?' Maisie's finger slid away from the button.

Katherine and I exchanged grins. 'This way will be much more fun.'

***

'How fortunate that there's another ball coming up so soon,' I said to Archie. 'And how odd that you didn't invite us.'

He squirmed in his seat. 'I don't get to choose,' he said.

'No,' said Katherine, thoughtfully. 'I don't suppose you do. And of course, given the tittle-tattle you've been spreading about my husband and I, we wouldn't be welcome at all, would we?'

Archie swallowed. 'That wasn't all me. That second piece wasn't me.'

'How do you think it felt to read those things?' Katherine asked, and her voice was dangerously quiet.

'I'm sorry, I was just —'

'I know. You were just following orders. Doing as you were told, like a good boy.' Archie wriggled like a pinned worm. 'And not caring whose life you wrecked so long as you stayed in favour with your master.'

Archie buried his head in his hands.

'What did you think would happen when you took people into the opium den?' asked Katherine. 'It's hardly a picnic by the Thames, is it?'

'I thought it was a bit of fun,' said Archie, rather indistinctly. 'You know, like a boys' club. An inner circle. A drink and a smoke away from the hoi polloi, a chat about business perhaps, an exchange of mutual favours —'

'So that's how you were recruited,' I said. 'An exchange of mutual favours. You do the dirty work, but in exchange for what?'

Archie frowned. 'Well, he never said in so many words, but I was given to understand that in the future, if all went well, there would be — preferment. Perhaps a sinecure somewhere, a little job with not much to do and the opportunity to make a bit on the side. You know the sort of thing.'

'I'm afraid I don't,' said Katherine. 'I spent years shut up in a typing room for five shillings a day.' Archie blushed. 'You utter fool,' she added.

'So,' I said, 'here's how I see things, Archie. You will give us your guest list, and we shall send out a few, shall we say, supplementary invitations. The theme of the event, please?'

'A pirate ball,' said Archie, sulkily.

'Excellent.' I made a note. 'The entertainment is all in

187

hand, I assume.'

'Oh yes, there will be a band playing sea shanties, and dancing.'

'Jolly good.' I made another note.

'And then there's going to be a —'

'Oh no there isn't,' I said. 'Whatever it is, you'll cancel it at the last minute.' I turned to Archie. 'And of course it is fancy dress.'

Archie nodded, his expression gloomy.

'Splendid. We shall arrange costumes. For you too, Archie.'

He swallowed. 'You're making me attend?'

'Oh yes,' I said. 'We couldn't run things without you, could we?'

Archie stared at me in utter horror, then his face crumpled into sobs. 'But then everyone will know!'

'Yes,' I said. 'Unmasking the horrible deception you've been caught up in is the point.'

Archie's head sank onto his arms and he began to cry noisily. Maisie leaned forward and lifted his chin so that he had to look at her. 'You have no choice, Archie. You've made your bed, and now you have to lie in it.' Her expression was almost a smirk. 'Take it like a man, dear.'

'One more thing,' I said. 'Your Masquerade Mob. What will they be wearing on this occasion?'

Archie snuffled for several seconds before he was composed enough to answer. 'Pirate rig,' he gulped. 'Black trousers and shirts, red-spotted neckerchiefs, tricorn hats, wooden swords, eyepatches.'

'That sounds entirely in order,' I said. 'You'll stand

them down at the last minute, too. Assiduous as they are, I think we should recruit a new team.'

'What are you planning, Connie?' asked Maisie, a gleam in her eye.

'Wait and see, Maisie,' I said, tapping my notebook. 'Oh, just wait and see.'

***

'Bravo!' I cried, applauding heartily as the 'Mob' bowed low. Albert and Maisie, beside me, were doing exactly the same. Archie sat, arms folded, glowering.

''Appy with that?' Mr Templeton called. 'We've done what we could for costumes but, well, short notice.'

'Of course I'm happy! It's all as I wanted.'

Mr Templeton frowned. 'I just 'ope they act as good as they look.'

'I trust them,' I said.

'But do you trust me?' asked Selina, tipping me a most piratical wink.

'I'd trust you with my life, Selina,' I replied. 'However, with a set of greasepaint sticks . . . I'm not so sure.'

Selina looked hurt. 'It'll all come off with a dab of —'

'I know,' I said. 'I was joking. Really.'

'Well, you'd best stir your peg leg, Captain,' she replied, grinning. 'We've the rest of you to fit out, and not too much time to do it in.'

***

'Are you sure everything's in place?' Katherine asked nervously. With her hair hanging down her back in a neat pigtail, she appeared no more than sixteen.

'Almost,' I replied. 'Everyone's ready and the advance

party have gone. There's just one more thing to do.'

Katherine looked resolute. 'Then let's do it.'

We took one last look at ourselves in the mirror. How I wished that Bee could have seen me. Then again, perhaps she might have cried.

'Stop admiring yourself,' said Katherine, nudging me.

'Oh, but I've never looked so beautiful,' I replied, and winked, I hoped in much the same style as Selina.

We left the quiet dressing room and met Albert and James in the corridor. 'What ho!' said James.

'Yo ho ho, you mean,' said Albert, examining his wooden sword critically.

'Oh, that too,' said James. 'Come along, the carriages are waiting. It would never do to be late for our own party.'

'True.' Albert sheathed his sword and offered me an arm. 'Shall we?'

Tredwell drove us across Lambeth Bridge and into Westminster, now quiet after the debates and arguments of the day. From Westminster we skirted Belgravia, passing close to Buckingham Palace, and I wondered what the Queen would say if she could see the troop of brigands so near her gates. Would she be amused, or not? We had been silent during the short ride, thinking over our part in the evening's duties, no doubt, or the strange series of events which had brought us to this place. In my mind was the whole sheet of stamps I had used, the plans we had made, the calls we had paid, and the conversations we had had.

'It won't fail, will it?' said Katherine, looking into my face.

I leaned across and squeezed her hand. 'Of course it

190

won't fail. *We* won't fail, Miss Caster.'

We passed the Wellington Arch, and Tredwell called 'Nearly there,' as if we didn't know. I gave Katherine's hand one more squeeze.

Park Lane was leafy, peaceful. Here and there the late-afternoon sun caught couples strolling, or glinted on the wheels of a perambulator. I thought of Bee and Lucy, sitting up and crowing in their chariot. I wanted both of them to be safe and happy, and never to have to face the things that we had seen in the last few weeks.

The carriage slowed. 'Here we go,' muttered James, and patted his pocket.

The other carriage was already there, and a group of pirates stood before us. Under the beards and eyepatches I could make out a telltale feature or two; round blue eyes, a slight stoop, a strand or two of white hair peeping out from beneath a hat...

'Ready?' I whispered, drawing my sword.

There was some shuffling and rustling, then a ragged chorus of 'Ready.'

I took a deep breath and summoned my confidence. 'Then off we go!' I stalked up the steps and rang the bell.

The door opened an inch. That was all I needed. I forced my foot into the gap.

'Good evening, madam!' I declaimed, as if I were addressing the back row of the music hall. 'We are the Masquerade Mob, and we have come to claim our prize!'

The pirates at the front put their shoulders to the door so forcefully that Phoebe had to jump back, her eyes round as crowns. 'Why, whatever —'

'Do not be afraid!' I boomed, as the Mob ran past me. 'You are not the one we seek!'

'Thank the Lord for that,' she said, and fell down in a faint. Katherine knelt beside her, and undid the button at her throat.

From the rear of the house came the bang of a door, followed by an irate 'What are you doing here?' Moments later the Mob ran Sir Joshua down the hallway, two men to each arm. His mouth was a hard line, his expression like a judge passing sentence. Inwardly I quailed; but them I remembered Bee, and stared straight back at him. Was that a gleam of recognition? Then he was gone.

Phoebe was beginning to stir, and Katherine stood up. 'Come on,' she said.

We found Alexandra standing perplexed on the landing, and when she saw us she screamed. 'It's all right!' I cried, in my normal voice. 'It's us. Connie and Katherine. Mrs Lamont and Mrs King.'

'Oh!' Her eyes were almost out of her head, her breath coming in gasps. 'I heard a frightful noise downstairs, so I came to see what was the matter. Why —'

'We're going to a ball,' I said.

Katherine moved forward carefully, as if Alexandra were a bird that might fly away, and took her hand. 'Do you remember when you wrote to me about Toby?'

She nodded, her thin frame absolutely rigid.

'Well, we have found out what happened.'

'Will you tell me?' she whispered.

Katherine hesitated. 'It may not be the answer you want. But we shall reveal the truth tonight. Do you wish to come, and hear it?'

Alexandra said nothing. Her eyes were focused on something beyond us, out of reach. She seemed to be listening to the silent house. Then she started, and when she turned to me her pale-blue eyes held a look of understanding. 'I think I have guessed,' she said, and her words had the weight of sureness behind them. 'I shall come. I can't stay alone here, waiting. Mother is sedated, and —'

'We shall look after you,' I said.

'But what shall I wear?' she exclaimed. 'I can't go like this! And I'm not invited —'

'Wait a moment.' I ran to the cab and returned with a Gladstone bag and our final member of the Mob. 'We brought this for you, and this gentleman will take you as his guest.'

The pirate lifted his eyepatch. 'I'm not sure if you remember me, Miss Arrington —'

Alexandra peered at him. 'Teddy?' she said. 'Teddy Gresham?'

'That's right,' said the pirate. 'Would you do me the honour?'

Alexandra stared for another second, then snatched the Gladstone bag from me and ran to her room. She rushed out three minutes later, sword-belt over her day dress, tricorn hat jammed on her head, and eyepatch askew. Teddy Gresham grinned, and offered her an arm. 'I am ready,' she panted, and towed him down the stairs.

Katherine and I exchanged glances. 'Then I think we are too,' said Katherine. 'Come on Blackbeard, let's go.'

Chapter 22
Katherine

We arrived at the Beaulieu and joined a line of carriages disgorging people in long cloaks and an abundance of tricorn hats.

Teddy Gresham sat opposite me and next to Connie, hands clenched in his lap. Alexandra sat beside me, quivering a little.

'Those four years at school were the happiest days of my life,' she said, very low. 'No-one was watching my every move. I even forgot to worry about Mother. I loved Geography best. I would look at the atlas and imagine worlds beyond my own. Do you know, when I heard that your father was missing and you decided to go out to work, I was jealous.'

'Most people looked down on me. All my old friends refused to receive my calls.'

'I didn't realise. I thought you were lucky, coming and going with no-one to care.'

'Life's not as simple as that, I'm afraid,' I said. 'There are different ways of being imprisoned. Alexandra, are you sure you want to come to the ball? It won't be like the last time you came. We —'

'I know.' She said nothing further, but reached across the carriage to Teddy and shook his hand as if making a pact. They both smiled before unclasping hands to don their masks.

We ascended the steps, handed our cloaks to the footmen and stepped into the ballroom, now festooned with ropes, fishing nets, and pirate flags.

James appeared, arm in arm with Maisie. I knew it was James as I'd drawn the jagged scar across his nose and glued on his sideburns myself, and the baffled-looking parrot on his shoulder had been made by an equally baffled Aunt Alice. Otherwise it would have been hard to tell. The guests had, to a large extent, dressed the same, having gone for costumes inspired by the most recent performance of *The Pirates of Penzance* and pictures from *Treasure Island*. Striped skirts, white frilled shirts, dark knickerbockers, tricorn hats and tropical birds abounded. Everyone sported a weapon of some description. Most were clearly fake, but one or two looked alarmingly as if they'd been plucked from a display in the family mansion.

There also seemed to be a great deal many more men than ladies.

Connie was not the only tall woman who had taken the opportunity to dress as a woman pretending to be a pirate captain. Like them, she wore a knee-length frilled white blouse over scarlet pantaloons. She was hatless, and her

195

hair was rolled to replicate men's fashion from around 1760 without the powder. Meanwhile, I was not the only small woman to be costumed as a cabin boy in a simpler version of Connie's outfit, my hair in a long braid tied with a black ribbon.

As we advanced I saw that the dais was set out like a deck complete with wheel, and on it stood Albert, tall and rakish in a tricorn hat, boots and sash.

The band fell silent and Albert's clear tones rang out. 'Good evening, ladies and gentlemen! Or should I say ahoy there, pirate kings and buccaneer queens!'

A cheer went up and fake swords bristled in the air like hedgehog spines.

'Welcome aboard the latest masquerade! An evening of intrigue, a board bursting with the finest wormy cheese, ship's biscuits and grog for our refreshment, and finally an entertainment the like of which you have never seen!'

'"Is this a dagger I see before me?"' quoted Connie under her breath. 'No it isn't. It's a sword. And I'm not afraid to use it! Avast there, Jim lad!' She leaned closer. 'All for one and one for all!'

'Whatever would your governess say if she heard you mixing up all that literature?' I whispered.

'She was a loathsome crustacean,' growled Connie. 'Keel-hauling would be too good for her. Besides, you can't call *Treasure Island* literature. It's not long been published. And she'd never have let me read it anyway.'

'And who knows?' Albert cried. 'Perhaps we may find treasure, unless of course that rascally Masquerade Mob turn the tables and demand ours! Let us cast off, and sail the seven seas to adventure!' He flung his arm in the air, waved his pistol and roared.

The band struck up a lively reel and the dancing commenced.

'I think you and Albert have truly found your niche,' I said, shaking my head in wonder.

'It'll be fun play-acting in the costumes at home later.' Connie smirked beneath her mask but contrived to go pink at the same time.

Before I could think of a reply, James bowed to me. 'May I have this dance, madam?' he asked, and whirled me off.

'Where is he?' I whispered.

'In a side room, fuming. He hasn't quite worked out what's happening, but he's keeping quiet.'

Once the first dance had ended I met Connie by a large vase of flowers and followed her until we were near the hidden door. She was shivering a little. I squeezed her hand. 'It'll be different this time,' I whispered.

In the air was a faint suggestion of the sickly scent which had been on Connie's clothes after the last ball, but I couldn't be certain. Then a strutting young pirate in blue stripes led one in red breeches past us. Blue-stripes was brandishing a pistol which, even in the dull light, appeared a little too battered to be a replica. Red-breeches was hanging back.

Blue-stripes spoke. 'Come on Travers, let's go and have some fun. This ball is jolly dull, but I know just the thing to perk it up. Just the *two* things, in fact.' He laughed.

'I'm not sure, Haynes,' said Travers. 'What sort of

things?'

'Experiences you'll never forget. Now give me that dagger, you don't want to scare the lady.'

'It's only wooden. And everyone's seen it already.'

Haynes laughed and shook his head. 'Not this lady. She's a *special* lady.'

'I don't think I —'

'Try everything once, old man. Come along.' He pushed aside the hangings, knocked a curious little knock and, when the door opened, led Travers in. From our vantage point I could see them open a second door, and make out, through a haze of smoke, a barely-dressed woman reclining on a divan. Connie shivered again, and the door closed.

A band of four pirates loitering in an alcove looked over. Two were wearing voluminous cloaks, and had a distinctly shifty air about them.

'Not yet, not yet,' whispered Connie. Then, a little more loudly, 'Now!'

The cloaked pirates whipped out cameras while the others rushed the door, splintering their way through it. Connie and I followed in their wake, past the quivering little attendant and through the second door. There was an explosion of light as a flash pan went off, then a silence as the smoke cleared, followed by the quiet click of a closing door. Our ears stopped ringing and our eyes adjusted. Travers was struggling to extricate himself from the grip of a woman who was holding a pipe in his mouth. Haynes was standing to the side with a camera half-hidden behind his back, and the other pirates had circled him. His mouth was opening and shutting as he looked for a way out.

'I didn't…' stammered Travers, finally pushing the woman away. 'It's not what it looks like. Please — my father —'

'It's all right, chum,' said one of the photographers. 'That's why we're here. Right then, you sneak,' he prodded Haynes. 'We have photographs of you preparing to blackmail this lad.'

'Th-that's not what it'll look like,' gabbled Haynes. 'There'll be three photographs of him smoking opium with a loose woman, instead of one.'

'Except that their photographs will be of you photographing him. And they'll be police evidence,' said another voice from behind us. 'Let me introduce myself. Chief Inspector Barnes. And you, the *Dis*honourable Bartholomew Haynes, are under arrest. Female in the slip and all of you pirates, honest or otherwise, you'll come out the back with me and answer some questions.' The two pirates who had broken down the door stepped forward and seized Haynes and the woman, who was trying to pull her shift over her exposed knees.

The Chief Inspector turned to me and Connie. 'Evening Miss Caster, Miss Fleet. I'll let you get on. Things are just getting interesting, aren't they?'

We slipped into the hall as a hornpipe was playing. The noise of the music and thumping feet was tremendous. The explosion of flash pans in the back room would have sounded like a moth's sneeze.

I surveyed the guests. Those who weren't dancing were milling about, conversing, flirting. Albert was near the dais, speaking with a pirate in checked breeches and a gold sash who was pacing as he talked, shaking his kerchiefed head.

'You looked better in polka dots, Miss C,' growled the gold-sashed pirate. 'And I thought you wouldn't wear trousis.'

'Mr Templeton!' I exclaimed.

'The very same, here to have a butchers for Smith. He's here, I can smell him. But so far I haven't seen the little runt.'

I scanned the room, even though I didn't know whom I was looking for. Alexandra, identifiable by her thinness and dress, stood a little to the back. She was twisting her hands but then her companion — surely Teddy — took one and tucked it in his arm. She turned her face up and smiled. Not far away I could see Maisie with a tall dark man; they were deep in conversation with a small group and Maisie threw her head back to laugh, her loose curls flowing over the laced bodice and past the waist of her blue striped skirt. Whether the tall dark man was mine or not was hard to tell across the ballroom.

'Stop staring at strange men,' whispered James in my ear and pulled my braid. Aloud he said, 'Where may a gentleman enjoy a cigar?'

'The smoking compartment has been shut,' I said.

'Good. Any particular reason?'

'It was full of newspaper men — you know how low they are — and they were startling a fluffy blonde woman with knobbly knees.'

Mr Templeton gave a low guffaw. 'Aha! Wild hair?

Innocent eyes? Knobbly knees? If that ain't Minnie Trott I'll eat my parrot. No judge in the country will believe a word she says. She's been in too many divorce courts as the co-respondent.'

Albert didn't smile. 'James? Any news?'

'No go. He's giving nothing away.'

Albert looked at me, then Connie. 'Are you sure about this?'

I bit my lip and studied Alexandra, who was approaching with Teddy.

James followed my gaze. 'I know what you're thinking but it's all right. When I spoke with Gresham she insisted on joining in. Don't worry.'

'What did the others say?' said Albert.

'Mostly yes,' said James.

'I'm in, Lamont,' said Gresham. His mouth was sober.

Alexandra beside him seemed frailer than ever, but she stood straight and tall as she turned to me. 'You think I'm mad wanting this, but I do. For justice.'

'Are you absolutely sure, K? Connie?' asked Albert.

We nodded.

***

We entered a side room to find Sir Joshua Arrington sitting back in his chair and perusing the Masquerade Mob, arms folded. His expression changed from a scowl to puzzlement as he looked Connie and me over. Then his eyes narrowed, and he stood up.

'Get those women out of here. I've told you already that I'm not stupid enough to get involved in the sort of thing you're describing. I have no idea what you're talking about, and I don't know what you're playing at. Bring me Smith, or I shall have the police on the lot of you.'

His fist clenched as he glared into my face.

'Ah, you're my daughter's old friend, Mrs King,' he said, with a sneer. 'The one with such a dubious husband. I wouldn't have sent Alexandra to that school, but her mother made such a fuss in public. Such a shame my wife became so poorly that her daughter had to come home.'

'And how did she become so ill?' I asked.

'Hysteria,' said Sir Joshua. He bent his head so that he was looking directly into my eyes, and it felt as if my mask was dissolving.

Two of the Mob, a tall one in a pirate outfit so sharp I wondered what Savile Row had made of the order, and a shorter one wearing something apparently lent by the music-hall, stopped leaning against the wall and stepped between me and Sir Joshua.

'I suggest you leave our cousin be,' said the taller pirate. It was Moss. A nervous cough from the other confirmed it was Nathan.

'Cousin?' Sir Joshua paused. Then, recovering himself, he turned his glare on Connie. 'And *you're* the tea-party guest. So sympathetic. I suggest you get out too before I lose my temper.'

'Sister-in-law,' said Moss. 'Suggest you don't.'

Sir Joshua ran his eyes round the Mob, and an unpleasant glint sparked in his eyes.

'You're not the same ones, are you?'

'Oh stow it, mate.' A cabin boy walked up close and jabbed his finger at Sir Joshua. Reg. 'Course we ain't. The trouble with toffs is they don't look properly at people they've hired, and they take too long to get to the point. The ladies've got evidence, see. Evidence to show what you've been doing. Blackmailing letters sent to people's homes. Copies of compromising photographs. Threats in dark alleys, rumours in the newspapers. Trying to ruin people like Mr King, and maybe murder too. Not very gentlemanly if you ask me, but then I'm not a gent. Now if you'll confess, then there needn't be any fuss. We'll help you along to the police station and —'

Sir Joshua threw his head back and laughed. 'And how do you connect any of that with me? What evidence? You have nothing.'

'Haynes is under arrest,' said Connie. 'He was caught trying to photograph Lord Edmund Travers in a compromising situation. Interesting, since Lord Edmund's father opposes a scheme which would make you even richer. Evicting the poor, destroying their homes, and providing expensive new accommodation which they will be forced to live in ten to a room. Oh, and clearing the area of all shops except the ones you get a cut from.'

Sir Joshua smirked. 'You can't prove one solitary thing, can you?'

'We can,' I said. 'We have statements from someone who worked closely with you.'

'I doubt it,' spat Sir Joshua.

'And some of your victims are willing to speak out.'

'Nonsense.'

'And —'

'I said nonsense. I'm not putting up with this any

203

longer.'

Before anyone could move, he sprang up and grabbed Connie, an open penknife held to her throat.

'No one move, or Captain Lamont will pay the price.' Using Connie as cover, he edged towards the door, opened it, shoved Connie forward and ran.

The Mob were after him like rats down a drain. Reg tackled Sir Joshua to the ground and twisted the knife away.

'You've had your chance,' said James. He hauled the baronet to his feet and with Albert's help dragged him onto the dais.

The band screeched to a halt and the whirling dancers tripped over each other as they tried to bring themselves to a stop. Sir Joshua stood defiant, the only one not in pirate attire. The expressions on the dancers' faces, as far as it was possible to tell from their mouths, ranged widely. To my surprise, few seemed genuinely confused. The remainder looked wary, resigned, angry. Alexandra was nowhere to be seen.

James removed his patch and took off his hat.

'I am James King,' he said. 'I grew up with many of you, went to school and university with some of you. You know me. I am a victim of this man's attempts to blacken my name, and now I am publicly accusing him. You know what I stand for. I say to you, Sir Joshua, that if you have any evidence to confirm what has been written about me, then publish it. I am not afraid.'

'How dare you accuse me?' snarled Sir Joshua. 'Who has any evidence linking me to any of this?'

'I have,' I said. James helped me up. I felt comfort from his warmth as I extracted Geraldine's letter from my pocket. 'This was written by a lady who posed as a loose woman as part of his scheme,' I said. 'The former society lady who died of an overdose recently. I beg that you listen to it all before making judgments on her. She too was a victim. It is addressed to her daughter.' I cleared my throat.

'My dear Lucy. I hope that you never read this; that I live to see you grow up, safe and happy and honourable. I was once such a lucky little girl. I had love, I had everything I could wish for, I did not have to raise a finger. My failing perhaps, was that I favoured luxury over anything else. The man I married was not a bad man. He was rich, and I was pretty. The only thing I wanted was a child and when it did not happen, I took desperate measures. This led to my downfall and my husband and my family rejected me.'

I paused and glanced up at the audience. There were mutterings and a few sniggers. Some probably thought this was all a play. Clearing my throat, I continued. *'They will not acknowledge you. I am sorry for this, my darling, but there is nothing I can do to change things. My brother made sure I had somewhere to live and a tiny allowance, provided I kept away, but I was not used to living in such low circumstances. No fine clothes, having to help with the housework, worrying whether I could afford to pay the bills. My requests for more help were met with silence.'*

Again I stopped. The masks made it impossible to read expressions, but there was something in the way people shifted that told me who felt pity and who felt contempt.

205

'One day, when I had no money and it was bitter winter, a man I met on the street, a Mr Smith, offered me "medicine" to relieve my distress. And I took it.'

This time I paused simply because I couldn't speak. I wondered if I would have done the same. How easy it must have seemed. 'Before too long, I could not manage a day without laudanum. I had to hand you to a baby farmer as I was often too insensible to care for you. Then, in time, he made me another offer: paid work. All I had to do was pretend to seduce young men, give them opium and allow myself to be photographed. I would be masked, I need not speak, I would be protected.'

Gasps rang around the room. Everyone was still motionless, listening.

'But I knew what I was doing was wrong, and that if it was ever discovered I would not be protected. So I collected evidence of my own. I pretended to be unconscious when I was not. That was when I saw Sir Joshua Arrington. I was lying on a divan when he came in to speak to Mr Smith, and when he saw my prostrate form he laughed. "How the mighty fall," he said. "Such a fine lady once, and now my handmaiden in disgrace. A nudge here, a resignation there, and when the Government falls, I shall have her to thank."

I shall leave this in a safe place, and should anything suspicious happen to me, I hope that it will be found. Forgive me, my darling. I am a foolish, sinful woman, but I loved you from the moment I knew you were coming to me.'

The silence when I finished was so profound that it hurt

my ears. I swallowed and looked up.

Teddy Gresham ascended the dais and stood beside James. 'I am a victim of this blackmail. I was one of those who entered the den, and I was sent photographs afterwards where I smoked an opium pipe, and appeared to carouse with a half-dressed woman. They would have disgraced my family. To my shame, my father resigned his seat in Parliament rather than expose me.'

Another man stepped forward. 'I am a victim, too.'

And another, and another.

'You're weak fools,' snapped Sir Joshua. 'Where is your self-control? Who will believe the letter of an addict, a disgraced woman, a —'

'My daughter.' A man in the crowd removed his mask and pushed his way to the front of the dancers. 'And I too, am a victim of yours. You told me that my daughter was a kept woman, and I let my pride stand in the way of my fatherly duty. And you a father of a daughter, too. How could you?'

'A daughter is a commodity. You should have managed yours better, Sir Christopher. I don't blame you for disowning her. Come, now.' Sir Joshua forced a smile onto his face and spread his hands, appealing to the crowd. 'My friends, most of you have known me your whole lives. Would you believe a sentimental journalist over me? Who's to say that woman wrote the letter at all? It was probably this scribbler!' He cast a contemptuous glance at James.

'I neither wrote the letter, nor did I investigate the crimes. For that, you have a certain Miss Caster and Miss

Fleet to thank,' said James with utter calm. 'But the police have all the evidence. This was your chance to face your peers before arrest.'

'Father.' Alexandra approached the dais. 'I have heard enough to give a statement. I do not care if I lose my reputation. You are a tyrant. You have always been a tyrant. You have made my life a living hell with your locked doors and marriage brokers, and you have destroyed my mother.'

Sir Joshua paled. 'Have you no shame? Go home.'

'I shall not. I shall testify against you, but first I want to know how you killed Geraldine Timpson.'

'I never laid a finger on the woman. I've never even seen her, and if she thought she saw me, she was mistaken. Her dealings were with Smith — find him, I say!' He flung an accusing finger at a short, squat man sidling towards the door. 'Look! There he is!'

'That's Smith all right,' bellowed Mr Templeton. 'I'd know him anywhere. Tried to corrupt my actresses, he did!'

Smith stopped dead, his hand in the inside pocket of his jacket. For two seconds, perhaps, he debated with himself. Then he withdrew his hand, and light caught the thin blade of his stiletto as he dropped it on the floor. 'John Smith's my name, and I'll answer to it,' he said, and the look on his face was ghastly. 'And I'll answer to what I was ordered to do, and not do. But I wasn't the one who got the Timpson woman into a cab, oh no. I wasn't the one who took her home, and gave her the draught that killed her, under the pretence of calming her down. I wasn't the one who made Langlands write a suicide note, then shot him. And I'll tell you who did —'

Sir Joshua twisted out of Albert's grip, drew a small revolver from an inner pocket, and fired. Smith fell to the ground, his fingers curling and uncurling as if trying to drag him towards his assailant.

Sir Joshua swept the gun round the room and the crowd drew back with a frightened murmur. Chief Inspector Barnes drew his gun, and aimed it. 'I advise you not to do anything stupid, Sir Joshua,' he said, and his eyes were like the twin barrels of his own gun.

'It was him, and I'll swear to it.' A fresh voice came from the side of the room. There, tricorn hat off, stood Archie Bellairs. He removed his eyepatch, and while his hand trembled, he stood firm.

'Sir Joshua made me promises, offered me a place at his right hand even, if I would help him. I placed slanderous notices in the papers. I sent invitations. I took people into the den.' Sir Joshua's revolver swung round. 'And I've already told the police everything I know.'

Sir Joshua's gun swung again, this time towards the side room where he had been confined. The crowd parted like a wave as he walked, his steps loud on the sprung wooden floor.

The door opened, then slammed behind him. Another shot rang out, followed by the sound of a body falling heavily to the floor.

CHAPTER 23
Connie

'It isn't quite what I had in mind,' I said, gazing about me from the vantage point of the tartan picnic rug. 'But it'll do.' The trees were tinged with autumn, but the temperature still warm summer.

'You've got water,' said Katherine, waving an arm at the boating lake. 'And grass.' She indicated the lawn, on which children were bowling hoops and throwing balls.

'Well yes, but I was thinking a picnic by the Thames, in a meadow —'

'I know. Have another sandwich.'

I rooted in the picnic hamper and unwrapped another packet. 'These are cheese, I think. Anyone?' James and Albert both raised a hand and I passed them a sandwich each.

'Excellent,' said James. 'Anyway, Katherine's managed a feat close to the impossible in finding a London park where none of us have been coshed, attacked or dumped after an attempted kidnapping.'

'Yet,' said Katherine, inspecting another packet of sandwiches. 'Ooh, cucumber. I think I shall.'

'So, how was it?' I asked.

Katherine took her time chewing her mouthful of sandwich. 'How was what?' she replied eventually, a little smirk at the corner of her mouth.

'Do I have to drag it out of you?' I laughed. 'The reason why we're sitting in Regent's Park and not by the Thames in Richmond, or Kew.'

'Oh, that.' Katherine took a provokingly large bite of her sandwich.

'If it makes you feel any better, Connie, she hasn't told me either,' said James.

'Maybe she got another telling-off,' I replied.

He grinned. 'Yes, maybe he rapped her over the knuckles with a ruler.'

'Or made her write one hundred lines,' said Albert.

'Or she had to stand in the corner with a book on her head —'

'All right, all right!' Katherine grinned, and put her sandwich on its paper. 'I went to see Lord Marchmont at the Department, as summoned, and...'

'And...?'

'He offered me my job back. Well, no, not quite. He offered me a promotion.'

'A promotion?' I hoped I sounded happy. I knew how upset Katherine had been when Mr Maynard had effectively dismissed her.

'Yes.' Katherine looked like a cat with a bowl of cream.

'A position in charge of a larger team, working on a wider range of cases. With my own administrative support.'

'That's wonderful,' I said. 'Congratulations, Katherine.'

Katherine's grin widened still further. 'And I turned it down.'

'What?' I goggled at her. 'I mean, I beg your pardon?'

'That's better.' She giggled. 'I thanked him, of course, but I said that my time away from the Department had shown me that I preferred working for myself.'

'What did he say to that?' asked James, taking another sandwich.

'Well, he was as straight-backed as ever, and he hummed and hawed a bit, but he said that he understood. So I gave him our card, and one to pass to Mr Maynard.'

'You didn't,' I breathed.

'I most certainly did.' Katherine drew a silver card-case from her handbag and flipped it open. '*Caster and Fleet Agency,*' she read. '*Discretion assured. Correspondence — care of Bayswater Road Post Office, London, W.* Perhaps, if things go well, we could even rent an office.'

I blinked. 'What did Lord Marchmont say? What did he do?'

'He said that he would have to consider the propriety of such an arrangement —'

'That's a surprise —'

'But in view of our previous unblemished — *unblemished* — work history with the Department, he would see what he could do.'

'Don't hold your breath,' cautioned James. 'The wheels of power move with glacial slowness. And there's nothing like an office for things being "accidentally" misfiled.'

'We know,' I said, rooting in the basket again. For some reason, discussing the Department always made me hungry.

I had expected a riot of arrests, accusations and counter-accusations after that fateful night at the Beaulieu Hotel, but there was only silence. I heard through Katherine, who had heard via Mr Maynard, that Lord Marchmont would lead an investigation, and then I heard no more. A small paragraph in the *Times* announced that the inquest into Sir Joshua Arrington's death had reached a verdict of death by misadventure. Shortly afterwards I had returned home to find Alexandra's card on the salver. Her Park Lane address was scratched out and *7 Albert Mansions, Victoria Street, Westminster* written in a pretty, flourishing hand beneath, with *At home Wednesday afternoons* added for good measure.

'It's so much nicer,' she exclaimed when I called. 'Everything's so cosy, and Mama and I have things the way we like them.' Her hands clenched a little, then relaxed. 'Mama has begun to go for drives in the park, and she is attending a lecture on the woman question this afternoon.' Her eyes gleamed. 'She is not quite her old self yet, but —'

'And how are you?' I didn't really need to ask Alexandra the question. Her movements were smoother, her little nervous habit of twisting her hands was gone, and she managed the heavy teapot without a tremor.

'Me? Oh, I'm quite well.' She set the teapot down, offered me the sandwich plate and then took two for herself. One disappeared in short order, then she smiled shyly at me, and her colour rose a little. 'Actually, I'm *very* well. Better than I've ever been.' I might have invited Alexandra to our picnic if I had not happened to know that she was lunching at Simpson's with Teddy Gresham. Oh, to have been a fly on the wall when Alexandra was faced with a Simpson's joint! And yet I had a feeling that with Teddy there, she would manage somehow.

Alexandra was not the only person to have moved on. I received a note in Maisie's dashing black hand: *Connie, come and see me. Friday a.m. best. M.* I arrived to find Maisie standing in a hallway full of boxes and crates and portmanteaux, waving her arms. 'No, not that one! *That* one! Isn't it obvious?' she cried, pointing to two identical boxes. 'Sorry, Connie,' she said, 'I just decided to get on with it.'

'Get on with what?' I asked, as two men in brown holland coats carried one of the boxes through the front door.

'I'm going abroad. Tea, please, Dora, in the study.'

I followed Maisie into her sanctum. 'This is rather sudden, Maisie.'

'It isn't, you know. I've been thinking about travelling abroad for a while. Men can travel, so why can't we?' Maisie sat in an armchair and waved me to the other one.

'Is it because of —'

'Archie? Good God, no. Well, not really.' Maisie looked pensive.

'It's all right to be upset, Maisie.' I reached over and took her hand.

The last I had seen of Archie Bellairs was when he was

214

marched away in the grip of a police officer. Later, when I made my statement to Chief Inspector Barnes, I enquired after Archie.

The Chief Inspector regarded me sternly. 'Now then, Connie, you should know better.' Then he grinned. 'He's a talkative young chap, is Mr Bellairs. A helpful soul. I believe his father is pulling strings.'

'He's in France.' Maisie's mouth quirked up a little at my startled expression. 'He wrote and told me.'

'Paris?' I could imagine Archie getting into trouble in Paris.

'Brittany. A quiet little fishing village. He's on bail, and he has to return the moment he's called.'

'Oh.' I looked at her. 'Is that where you're going?'

'No!' Her laughter was loud in the quiet room. 'I'm travelling to the East. I have my letters of introduction, and as you've seen, I'm nearly packed. I leave tomorrow morning.'

I stared at her. 'You're going alone?'

Her eyes met mine. 'Yes.' Her gaze wavered a little, then steadied. 'Archie used me, I know that. I think I knew it at the time, but —' She shrugged. 'I enjoyed it. Of course he's apologised, and promised never to do it again, and sworn on the life of everyone he can think of . . . but that isn't the life I want. I'd rather be alone, and steer my own ship.' She looked down, then smiled. 'I'll send you accounts of all my adventures. Perhaps Mrs King's father can make a book of them.'

I smiled back. 'He'd probably want to come with you.'

Maisie assumed a severe expression. 'Oh no, I can't

have that. I shall be magnificently independent and free of men.' Her frown dissolved. 'Perhaps not always. But certainly for now.'

'Ow!' I glared at Katherine, who had just dug me in the ribs.

'I had to get your attention somehow,' she replied, smirking. 'We've been calling your name for the last two minutes. I even waved a ham sandwich in front of your face, and there wasn't a flicker.'

'I was thinking,' I said, drawing myself up as straight as you can when you're sitting on the ground. 'Anyway, what is it?'

'I have news,' said James, lying propped up on one elbow on the other rug.

'Ooh, tell us!' I exclaimed, all attention. 'Are you back at the *Chronicle*?'

'Yes, but that isn't it. Try again.'

'You've taken Mr Templeton up on his offer at last, and you're going to be a magician at the Merrymakers?'

James snorted. 'I'd love to, but you're still wrong.'

'I have it,' said Albert. 'You'll take over Hazelgrove and farm pigs.'

'I can see I'll have to tell you,' said James. 'I . . . am going to be an editor.' Next to him, Katherine's face shone with pride.

'Of a newspaper?'

James beamed. 'Yes. It'll be more of a free sheet at first, but in time… It came about through a conversation with Mr Harper. Katherine's cousin's father-in-law,' he said, in answer to my puzzled expression.

'That's much clearer. Do go on.'

'He's a printer with considerable interest in workers' rights and humane treatment for the poor. I'm a journalist who specialises in that very thing, and at that point I was without a paper to write for.'

'The perfect match,' said Katherine, squeezing his arm.

'Indeed.' James leaned across and kissed her until he was in considerable danger of overbalancing. 'We shall call it *The Worker's Voice*, and report on things that the working classes ought to know. We'll translate what all the hot air in Parliament actually means for them. I've called in some favours at the *Chronicle*, and Mr Harper has already lined up reporters to give us accounts of the rallies and meetings they attend — Katherine's cousin Nathan and his wife are among them. I'm hoping that in time I can step back and let one of them run the paper.'

'That's wonderful news,' I said, and this time I meant it wholeheartedly.

'It certainly is,' said Albert. 'And if you need any additional backing —'

'Oh, I have some seed money.' James patted his waistcoat. 'I wrote to a certain Liberal peer of our acquaintance who has interests in newspapers, and he has pledged his support.'

'Lord Marchmont will be a very busy man,' I said. 'What with employing us, and overseeing James, and prolonging his investigation until everything's firmly swept under the carpet, and entertaining my parents to dinner —'

Katherine's eyebrows shot up. 'Is he?'

'Oh yes. Lady Marchmont called on Mother and

apologised for her, um, misunderstanding of the situation.'
I grinned. 'Mother told me that she considered inventing a
prior engagement, just to make her point, but she's going. I
believe she's ordering a new dress for it.'

'So everyone will live happily ever after,' said James,
rummaging in the bag he had brought with him and
extracting a bottle of champagne and four glasses wrapped
in napkins. 'And on that note…'

'I did wonder what you had in there,' said Katherine, as
he handed us each a glass.

'Well, my pirate outfit's at the bottom, but that's for
later.' James popped the cork and filled our glasses, the
wine fizzing to the brim before subsiding. 'I propose a
toast. To new ventures!'

'To new ventures,' we echoed, and clinked glasses. I
sipped the champagne and a delicious bubbling chill of
possibilities coursed through me. I closed my eyes and saw
an office with a telephone, and a kettle, and someone else
to do the typing while Katherine and I solved cases and
apprehended criminals —

'What are you thinking?' murmured Albert.

'Oh, just dreaming of the future,' I replied. 'You?'

'Likewise,' he said. He leaned forward to kiss me, and I
put my face up to his. And out of the corner of my eye I
saw James and Katherine doing exactly the same.

Acknowledgements

First of all, thank you to our beta readers — Ruth Cunliffe, Stephen Lenhardt, and Val Portelli — and our super-speedy proofreader John Croall. We couldn't do it without you! We would throw a masquerade ball for you all, but we're too tired from creating the fictional version! Any errors remaining in the book are of course the responsibility of the authors.

While we looked up all sorts of things in the course of writing this book (camera sizes, flash photography, small guns, the history of PO boxes…), there are just a couple of resources we'd like to cite here:

'The Victorian Baby: 19th Century Advice on Motherhood and Maternity' by Mimi Matthews: https://www.mimimatthews.com/2016/05/08/the-victorian-baby-19th-century-advice-on-motherhood-and-maternity/

London in the Nineteenth Century: A Human Awful Wonder of God by Jerry White: https://www.goodreads.com/book/show/2540781.London_in_the_Nineteenth_Century

And finally, thank you for reading! We never expected to be writing the afterword for book four less than a year after the first words of book one, and we're very happy and excited that people are joining us on the journey! We hope you've enjoyed Katherine and Connie's latest adventure, and if you could leave the book a short review — or a star rating — on Amazon or Goodreads we'd be very grateful.

Font and image credits

Fonts:

Main cover font: Birmingham Titling by Paul Lloyd (freeware):
https://www.fontzillion.com/fonts/paul-lloyd/birmingham

Classic font: Libre Baskerville Italic by Impallari Type (http://www.impallari.com): https://www.fontsquirrel.com/fonts/libre-baskerville License — SIL Open Font License v.1.10: http://scripts.sil.org/OFL_

Vector graphics:

Mask (texture and slight colouring added): at SVG Silh: https://svgsilh.com/image/3264409.html (adapted from an original image at pixabay.com). License: CC0 1.0 (public domain): https://creativecommons.org/publicdomain/zero/1.0.

Swords (recoloured): Sword and Scabbard at Wikimedia Commons, from a collection at Auckland Museum: https://c o m m o n s . w i k i m e d i a . o r g / w i k i /

About Paula Harmon

At her first job interview, Paula Harmon answered the question 'where do you see yourself in 10 years' with 'writing', as opposed to 'progressing in your company.' She didn't get that job. She tried teaching and realised the one thing the world did not need was another bad teacher. Somehow or other she subsequently ended up as a civil servant and if you need to know a form number, she is your woman.

Her short stories include dragons, angst ridden teenagers, portals and civil servants (though not all in the same story — yet). Perhaps all the life experience was worth it in the end.

Paula is a Chichester University English graduate. She is married with two children and lives in Dorset. She is currently working on a thriller, a humorous murder mystery and something set in an alternative universe. She's wondering where the housework fairies are, because the house is a mess and she can't think why.

Website: www.paulaharmondownes.wordpress.com
Amazon author page: http://viewAuthor.at/PHAuthorpage

Books by Paula Harmon

Murder Britannica

When Lucretia's plan to become very rich is interrupted by a series of unexpected deaths, local wise-woman Tryssa starts to ask questions.

The Cluttering Discombobulator

Can everything be fixed with duct tape? Dad thinks so. The story of one man's battle against common sense and the family caught up in the chaos around him.

Kindling

Is everything quite how it seems? Secrets and mysteries, strangers and friends. Stories as varied and changing as British skies.

The Advent Calendar

Christmas as it really is, not the way the hype says it is (and sometimes how it might be) — stories for midwinter.

Weird and Peculiar Tales (with Val Portelli)

Short stories from this world and beyond.

About Liz Hedgecock

Liz Hedgecock grew up in London, England, did an English degree, and then took forever to start writing. After several years working in the National Health Service, some short stories crept into the world. A few even won prizes. Then the stories started to grow longer . . .

Now Liz travels between the nineteenth and twenty-first centuries, murdering people. To be fair, she does usually clean up after herself.

Liz's reimaginings of Sherlock Holmes, her Pippa Parker cozy mystery series, and *Bitesize*, a collection of flash fiction, are available in ebook and paperback.

Liz lives in Cheshire with her husband and two sons, and when she's not writing or child-wrangling you can usually find her reading, messing about on Twitter, or cooing over stuff in museums and art galleries. That's her story, anyway, and she's sticking to it.

Website/blog: http://lizhedgecock.wordpress.com
Facebook: http://www.facebook.com/lizhedgecockwrites
Twitter: http://twitter.com/lizhedgecock
Goodreads: https://www.goodreads.com/lizhedgecock

Books by Liz Hedgecock

Short stories
The Secret Notebook of Sherlock Holmes
Bitesize

Halloween Sherlock series (novelettes)
The Case of the Snow-White Lady
Sherlock Holmes and the Deathly Fog
The Case of the Curious Cabinet

Sherlock & Jack series (novellas)
A Jar Of Thursday
Something Blue
A Phoenix Rises (winter 2018)

Mrs Hudson & Sherlock Holmes series (novels)
A House Of Mirrors
In Sherlock's Shadow (2019)

Pippa Parker Mysteries (novels)
Murder At The Playgroup
Murder In The Choir
A Fete Worse Than Death
Murder In The Meadow

Caster & Fleet Mysteries (with Paula Harmon)
The Case of the Black Tulips
The Case of the Runaway Client
The Case of the Deceased Clerk
The Case of the Masquerade Mob